A CHANCE TO LOVE

FAMILY MATCHMAKER
BOOK ONE

SUMMER COOPER

LOVE BOOKS LTD

Lovy Books Ltd
20-22 Wenlock Road
London N1 7GU

Cover by SC Creative

1

—————

$\mathcal{I}$ hated him instantly. Granted, I didn't really know him. But everything I knew about him already bothered me, from his cocky walk to his condescending treatment of every employee he'd already met. Word had traveled fast that he was a jerk. He'd only been in the building for a little over an hour but it felt like an eternity since everyone, including myself, was tense and on edge because of his presence. I wondered if he knew he made all of us uncomfortable, but as he approached it was clear from the look of self-satisfaction on his face that yes, he knew he made us uneasy, and he was enjoying it.

I watched him approach and sighed in resignation. I guess I was next. I didn't even pretend to be working. My shift was ending in ten minutes and it had already been a slow day. And since I was a customer service rep that meant I'd already spent hours on end trying to look busy.

He had squinty eyes, a bulbous nose, and barely perceptible lips. He looked like he drank heavily and slept rarely. His physical appearance didn't concern me. What concerned me was the way he looked at me with that stupid smirk on his face, as if he knew a cutesy little secret about me that he just couldn't wait to taunt me about. He was just so creepy, and I could tell he was going to be a pain in my backside, but I smiled tightly as he approached, took a deep breath and tried to fix the expression on my face so that I looked at least a little bit personable.

Maybe I was wrong. Maybe he would be nice. And then his eyes fixed on my breasts for a moment too long and I groaned. I had a bad habit of giving people the benefit of the doubt and second-guessing my instincts. Terry Baxter, our new store manager, apparently didn't deserve the benefit of the doubt. And for the record, he was again looking at my boobs. Looked like I was going to be looking for a new job this evening. I was seriously kicking myself for the bad life choices I'd made that had led to me working as a customer service rep at Primrose Grocery Store and Outlet.

I felt a little sad. I'd kind of liked working at Primrose. Everyone was really nice including the previous store manager, Mr. Jeffries, who Terry Baxter was replacing. Mr. Jeffries had been fired for being a little bit tipsy on the job and flashing a customer who had become difficult and refused to leave even though the store was closing. Apparently, the customer had not appreciated seeing our manager's pale butt cheeks and had contacted our corporate office to complain.

The next day we were all called into the conference room and as expected Mr. Jeffries wasn't there. Instead, someone from corporate greeted us and informed us that Mr. Jeffries was no longer employed by the company. Then we'd all been forced to sit through training on appropriate employee relations before being informed that a new store manager would be visiting us later in the week. We'd all groaned and vocalized our objections, but corporate's stooge had said that Primrose Grocery Store didn't have room in its culture for flashers, yet here I was being ogled by Mr. Jeffries's replacement. I was angry; I would miss the old manager. Yeah, he'd mooned someone, but he'd always been kind to me. He'd been flexible and understanding and had given me, a single mom with little work experience, a way to provide for my daughter. Flasher or not, to me he had been a saint, a godsend.

"Dana," said my department manager, a handsome Pakistani man in his late sixties who had worked at Primrose since the store opened nearly forty years ago. "This is Terry Baxter, our new store manager. And Mr.

Baxter, this is Dana, our brightest and most punctual customer service rep."

I was kind of flattered that Mo had said I was punctual. I busted my butt to get to work on time and prided myself on being a morning person. Granted, I was only a morning person after two or three cups of coffee.

Quickly, I forgot about Mo's compliment as Mr. Baxter's eyes settled on me. He gave me a creepy little smile before extending his hand. He had fat fingers with a few open sores across his knuckles.

What was he? Some sort of cage fighter at night? Or—oh God—was that herpes? Did people get herpes on their hands? I made a mental note to wash my hands a bajillion times as I let him take my hand in his. I tried to smile back but there was no use. I had the type of face that didn't hide emotions well. Any barely perceptive person could read my emotions just by glancing at me. And I was sure my face read, "Don't touch me, don't look at me, and please don't speak to me."

I pulled my hand away since apparently, Mr. Baxter was in no hurry to break contact. Mo didn't notice. He continued talking while I resisted the urge to wipe my hand on my jeans. I felt icky.

"Mr. Baxter will be around checking in on us from time to time and probably talking a little bit to our customers. He just wants to get a feel for the place and our current operation."

I nodded, grunted, and reluctantly tried to smile again. Mo noticed my expression and frowned a bit. Apparently, my smile was unconvincing.

"Are you feeling okay, Dana?" he asked. Before I could come up with a plausible excuse for why I couldn't do anything but frown in Mr. Baxter's presence, we were interrupted.

"Excuse me for a second," Mo said tightly as a group of teenagers rowdily entered the store, knocking over a patron. Mr. Baxter and I watched as Mo hurriedly assisted the fallen customer while admonishing the teens who looked on indifferently.

Once Mo was out of earshot, Mr. Baxter laughed. "I barely understood a word that guy said."

My eyes narrowed. And apparently, Mr. Baxter was also a bigot. Mo spoke perfect English. After all, he had been born and raised in Toledo, Ohio.

"I understand Mo just fine."

Mr. Baxter made a 'tssk' sound and then said, "Immigrants. I don't know why Primrose hires so many."

I saw red but managed to control my temper. "Umm... my parents were Croatian immigrants. I'm a first-generation American."

He wrinkled his nose in confusion. "Croatia? Where's that? Is that in Russia?" He then apparently grew bored of talking geography and glanced to where Mo was trying to appease the customer who had taken a spill. "That old fart needs to watch where she's going next time."

I stiffened. "The teenagers were at fault, not Mrs. Bailey. She's a pretty loyal customer, by the way. I hope this incident doesn't make her reconsider shopping here."

He shrugged. Clearly, he didn't care about customer loyalty. "Aren't you sweet, Dana?" he said mockingly. "It's going to be a pleasure to work with you I'm sure."

His eyes went to travel down my body again. The nerve of the man. He didn't even try to be subtle.

"My eyes are up here," I growled. *God, he was sleazy.* I gave up pretending his sleaziness didn't bother me. I'd resigned myself to looking for another job anyway as soon as he had approached me.

Mr. Baxter smiled. "I like feisty women."

"Too bad. I'm not into pervs who abuse their power." *Where had that come from?* I was on a roll today. I even surprised myself!

His expression instantly changed. Uh oh, I thought. I'm about to be fired. But I wasn't going to back down. I'd spent almost the last decade of my life being a doormat. I needed to grow a backbone, starting now.

His thin lips pulled back into a sneer and he looked at me as if I were a disgusting piece of gum stuck to his shoe.

"Insubordination is a fireable offense."

"So is sexual harassment," I shot back.

His demeanor instantly changed. His eyes darkened in anger and he growled, "I'd be careful if I were you."

My heart was pounding and I could feel sweat pouring down my back. I hated confrontation, but ever since my divorce, it was like I couldn't help but get confrontational. Maybe I was a bitter divorcee, snapping at everyone. But this guy deserved it. He wasn't a good person. He didn't respect me, and he'd thought that he could intimidate me. I wasn't going to let him.

"I'm sorry, that took longer than expected..." Mo's voice trailed off as he looked from me to Terry. I hadn't even noticed he'd come back.

"Everything okay?" he asked with uncertainty. Mo was a good guy, but he hated confrontation even more than I did. There was no way I was going to get him involved. If Terry continued to objectify me, I would just report him to corporate, not that I planned to stay at Primrose much longer.

Terry shot me a warning look and gave Mo a big fake smile before clamping him hard on his shoulder as if they were buddies.

"Everything's fine. Ms. Dana here and I were just getting to know each other—"

"It's missus not miss. Mrs. Dana Duran." Technically that was a lie since I was no longer married, but he didn't need to know that my husband had divorced me.

And the last name was mine. My ex had taken everything else, but I was determined to keep the name. I'd earned it. I'd been a devoted wife for seven years.

"Mrs. Duran, then," he said through clenched teeth. "You should get back to work. A line is forming. Work is what we pay you to do, right?" He turned away without another word. Mo shot me an apologetic look and jogged to catch up with him.

I sighed to myself wondering what I'd done so wrong in a past life that the universe wanted to punish me by making me broke and lonely, and now I was at the mercy of a total creep. The universe just wasn't fair.

Nearly a year ago I'd been leading the perfect suburban housewife existence. I had disposable income, a 3000 square foot home, a three-car garage, and a swimming pool. Now, at the ripe old age of twenty-seven, I was struggling financially and I didn't know where my life was going. I lived in a tiny home with my kid that barely had a backyard let alone a swimming pool.

I rolled my shoulders a few times in an attempt to de-stress. I tried to count my blessings and think of all the things I was grateful for, but I was in too much pain to focus on being positive. My shoulders hurt. My back hurt. And I was starting to get a headache courtesy of my encounter with the creepy new manager. It was hard to believe that almost a year ago I'd been happy. Unemployed but happy. I'd only been unemployed because my husband had told me that I didn't need to work, that I could trust him to take care of us and I'd trusted him. And at the end of the day he had taken all the money he'd earned, divorced me and married a nineteen-year-old. Trust in a marriage was clearly overrated.

"Hi, how can I help you?" I said to the next customer. I was doing my job, but my head was elsewhere. I was in a full-blown pity party because my encounter with Terry Baxter had really rattled me. I probably needed to see a therapist, not that I could afford one, but I felt I spent every moment since Tom had told me he wanted a divorce, expecting the figurative "other shoe" to drop. But things did seem to have gone from bad to worse over the past eleven months.

Life was hard. And maybe I was just a spoiled whiner, but I couldn't help but compare my life then to my life now. I'd been a stay at home wife for seven years and a stay at home mom for five of those years.

I'd been really happy. And to be honest, I hadn't missed working. Before marrying Tom, my only work experience had been as a cashier anyway. I tried to ignore the irony that eight years later, post-college degree, I was working pretty much as a cashier again.

When I'd tried to get back into the workforce after I realized that Tom was definitely serious about getting divorced and there was nothing I could do to stop him,

I'd tried to get a job in marketing. After all, my degree was in marketing. To my surprise, I was vastly under-qualified. Even with my fancy degree from a fancy school, I knew nothing about digital marketing which is what all the firms I applied to wanted. My knowledge of social media marketing strategies was nonexistent. I didn't get one call back.

"Thanks, and have a great day," I said with a forced smile as I finished up with the customer. My shoulders still hurt, and I watched as the woman I'd just helped exited the store. A family came in as she exited. It was a woman about my age, with a son around five years old. I could tell from their clothes and her expensive handbag and shoes that her socio-economic status was similar to what mine had been. I figured she was another stay-at-home mom. Hmmm, I thought to myself, maybe she'll be lucky and her husband won't leave her for a nineteen-year-old.

It's funny, but the way I found my first job, post-divorce, was exactly by shopping. When I tried to make a purchase on my husband's debit card and it was denied, I'd been in a Primrose Grocery Store and the cashier who had seen me shopping there for years, had kindly mentioned that the grocery store was hiring. I guess everyone had heard I was divorced. I'd lived in a small town and it was true that word traveled fast.

Up until that moment, I think I'd still been in denial.

I'd been spending money irresponsibly as if Tom was still footing all the bills. It had been a shock when our joint account had no money in it. I'd cried then, right in front of the cashier and that's when I'd met Mr. Jeffries who was visiting from a store in the city. He had taken me into his office and offered to pay for my groceries and then offered me a job.

We'd talked forever. It turned out that he too was going through a bitter divorce. I'd still been in denial that my divorce had been anything but amicable, so I'd felt sorry for Mr. Jeffries. He, in turn, had felt sorry for me. Mr. Jeffries's wife of thirty-four years had left him. She woke up one day, told him that she had never wanted to get married or have kids. Mr. Jeffries recounted to me that he had stared at her in shock. Not only had they been married since their twenties, but they'd had five kids together.

Mr. Jeffries had then told me that his wife had moved to Vegas and had become a lounge singer and that she was really happy while he was absolutely miserable and lost without her. We'd bonded over the feeling of being lost, thrown away, and depressed. He'd hired me on the spot.

That night, I packed the last of my stuff from the house I'd shared with Tom and our daughter. I'd packed my tiny car to the rooftop and had driven straight to the city. I'd rented a hotel suite at the last minute in a sketchy part of town just so that I could figure out my next move. Through the thin walls, I could hear a couple arguing next door and I could smell the funk of boiled cabbage in the air.

My daughter had handled the move swimmingly. She was a ball of enthusiasm even though everything in her life was changing. As she'd lain next to me sleeping that night, I'd cried silently for the life that I'd lost. I cried for my daughter who was now from a broken home. I cried for all the things I wouldn't be able to give her. I didn't know how I would pay for our next meal let alone her college tuition in thirteen years.

My parents had offered to let me live with them, but I wasn't interested. Their marriage had been more dysfunctional than mine. In hindsight, they were probably the reason I married the first man who was nice to me. My dad had been mostly absent, and my mom was a narcissist who always played the victim. I'd escaped their household and was not looking to go back. And they didn't believe in divorce. When I'd first told them what was happening, they were upset but kept pushing me to work it out with Tom. Finally, one night, I remember yelling, "There's no working anything out. He doesn't love me anymore, okay? He wants out! He just doesn't love me!"

My dad had scoffed, "Marriage isn't about love. It's about duty."

Mom had visibly winced at Dad's words and for the first time in a long time, my heart went out to her. She was in a loveless marriage. Maybe that's why she was so nasty to me growing up. Dad hadn't been mean, just vacant. Even when he was home, he had been on the phone with customers or just absent emotionally. He answered questions from me with monosyllabic words and never showed up to any of my events at school unless his boss was going to be there too.

It was no wonder that I didn't notice my own marriage was falling apart given how my parents had rarely spoken to each other, I thought that was normal for all marriages. I thought Tom was content playing his role and I was content playing mine. Apparently, he had wanted more. Or maybe he had just wanted younger.

But who was I kidding? Tom hadn't been very interested in me since we'd first gotten married. The first two years of Meredith's life were a blur to me because I'd been so sleep deprived. She had been a colicky baby and hated bedtime. I'd had no help. Tom had been like an absentee dad. It wasn't until Meredith was three years old that he'd taken an interest in her and they'd been inseparable ever since. He had more than adequately made sure she was cared for during and after our divorce proceedings. He paid her private school tuition and paid child support, but I was on my own otherwise. Hence his debit card had no funds on it. I guess he didn't think paying for food was necessary.

The Primrose Grocery store chain that I worked for was local and family owned. The pay was laughable but the benefits were great. Mr. Jeffries had been generous enough to let me work eight hours in split shifts so I had time to drop Meredith off at school and pick her up. Sometimes her father arranged a transportation service for her, but I still preferred to pick her up whenever I had time.

Adjusting to my new life had been hard. And sadly enough, I still missed my ex-husband. Well, actually, I'm not sure if I missed Tom or the life he represented. But what did it matter? He had moved on while I was still dealing with feelings that alternated between anger and bitterness. I'd said a lot of things I regretted, but I'd meant them. But knowing that I was still hung up on our divorce while he had easily replaced me made me feel sad and worthless.

I didn't know what to expect when he eventually moved on and he had moved on quickly. Our divorce was barely final before he married a nineteen-year-old blonde. I was in shock, but I'm not sure why. He was handsome. He was loaded. And everyone, excluding those that knew him really well, thought he was a great guy. A great guy that hadn't wanted me. I was angry. But I would get over it. Maybe. It had been nearly a year since my divorce and I still hadn't gotten over it.

I was so deep in thought that I hadn't noticed my shift had been over for at least twenty minutes already.

"I'll see you later, Lucy," I called to my fellow customer service rep as she moved to take my spot.

"Same time, same place," she called back giving me a wave.

I waved back and headed to the area where we kept our lockers and personal effects. I opened my locker, grabbed my purse and hustled for the exit. I waved to another friend as I did, "I'll see you later, Patrick."

Patrick was an older African-American man who worked there greeting customers. I'd heard he'd held that same job for at least twenty years.

"See you later, Dana. Try to not have too much fun tonight," he said with a smile.

"We definitely don't have to worry about that, Patrick. I'm not doing anything fun."

He gave me a teasing smile, "Don't I know it."

I laughed at his quick wit and headed out into the fresh air. It was April in Ohio and colder than usual. I was glad I didn't live too far from work. My parents had given me one of their rental properties as a wedding gift years ago.

Tom had wanted me to sell it, but I hadn't. Now I was grateful I'd stuck to my guns. I'd rented it out while

I'd been married and had managed to pay the mortgage off. After our divorce, it seemed the most logical thing to do was to live in it. No matter how much I'd wanted to stay in our town, it had made more sense to live in the city where life was kind of crazy but a lot cheaper than the ritzy town where I'd lived before my divorce.

It was a ranch style home, modest and practical. I was thankful it belonged to us. The '70s wallpaper was hideous, and the bathroom had pink tiles, but I was grateful I didn't have to worry about a mortgage. If it hadn't been for that house, I would have probably been still living in a hotel or in a crappy apartment somewhere just barely surviving on public assistance.

I pushed those thoughts out of my head as I pulled up to the school and saw Meredith, my daughter, standing there with a tall man with long hair. As I pulled closer, I realized that I knew the man she was with all too well. His name was Carter Knight and once upon a time, before I'd made a mistake that I would always regret, he had been my best friend.

2

"Uh oh," I said to myself. I hoped she wasn't in trouble. Meredith was a good kid, but she was rambunctious and strong-willed. I joked that she got that from her father, but I was lying. She was totally a little me.

I got out the car and smiled at Carter as I approached. It was so good to see him again. How long had it been? Seven, eight years? Too long. Way too long.

"Principal Knight," I said formally. "Is my daughter in trouble?"

He laughed. "Meredith did not inherit her mother's troublemaker genes."

"That's a relief."

We stared at each other, smiling. I'd met Carter in college. He'd lived a few doors down from me in the dorm during our freshman year. We'd instantly become friends. It had been the three of us: me, Piper, and Carter. Piper had been my roommate and was also Tom's little sister. In fact, I'd met Tom through Piper. We'd all gone to the same college, but Tom had been a senior when the rest of us had been sophomores. Tom had never liked Carter. And I'd suspected, even though Carter never said anything, that the feeling had been mutual.

Piper, Carter and I had hung out all the time. We'd been a dynamic trio. At least, that's what we told each other. They had been my best friends. I was able to stay in touch with Piper because I'd married her brother, but unfortunately, I hadn't kept in touch with Carter over the years. I'd heard from Piper that he had done a lot of volunteer work abroad while earning his PhD in some esoteric subject. But he had a teaching degree and had returned to our city just a few months ago and had accepted the principal position at the private school where Meredith was enrolled. It was an international private school, so lots of kids there were from other places. From what I understood, it was the perfect position for Carter.

I felt sort of bad that my work schedule had prevented me from ever meeting up with him in the three months since he'd been at Meredith's school. I only knew he worked there because of the letter that was sent home to all the parents.

I studied him as my brain tried to make sense of the man in front of me who was no longer the boy I knew. He was tall with broad shoulders. He tanned easily unlike my ex who burned within seconds. I sighed. I was still comparing others to Tom. That wasn't good, I told myself.

Carter had an easy smile and he surprised me by picking me up and spinning me.

"Carter! Carter! Put me down," I yelled through giggles.

He finally did and then hugged me tight.

"I'm sorry. I'm a jerk. Did I make you sick?" he asked, pulling away from me with his hands still on my shoulders.

"Maybe. I'm not sure yet," I said feeling a little wobbly, but more exhilarated than I'd felt in a very long time. "It's so good to see you," I said truthfully. "It's been years. You look great... very happy." I wasn't just saying that. He looked like he hadn't aged at all. He had the same cheerful demeanor and easy-going vibe. Clearly, he wasn't a struggling divorcee. Not that he had ever married... I think. Piper would have told me if he had gotten married, right? I subtly tried to look at his hand to see if he wore a ring.

He was still smiling, revealing a cute dimple in one cheek. "Thanks. It's easy to maintain a proper diet when all you have around you is pretty much fruit and vegetables."

He slowly released my shoulders and held my hands. He couldn't stop smiling at me and that made me blush even though we'd known each other for such a long time.

Carter had grown up. He still had that youthfulness about him, but he looked more mature. When he had once been gangly and kind of scrawny, he'd filled out, becoming much more muscular.

His face was the same. He had dark brown hair and arresting green eyes. Women had practically fallen over him in college and he'd ignored most of them. He'd been all about studying and helping others. Instead of keg parties, he did community service. Instead of studying abroad to get drunk in Paris, he'd studied abroad in developing nations helping with underserved communities. Carter had practically been a saint.

He'd been focused, goal-oriented, and as a result, had achieved more in his lifetime than most people his age. His success intimidated me given where I currently was in life.

He'd traveled the world and done amazing things. I only could take credit for being a divorced, single mom, cashier. My existence wasn't even good enough to be called mediocre.

He'd been in town for at least three months and I

hadn't seen him once. Meredith and Piper frequently saw him, but I never seemed to find the time. I added terrible friend to my list of failures.

I gave him a big smile and said truthfully, "It's great to see you again."

He continued holding my hands and surprised me by saying, "You look great."

I was still sexy, thank goodness. I'd let myself go a little while I was married and had started looking a little frumpy, if I were truthful with myself. I'd lost forty pounds during the past year because I'd been so stressed about the divorce that I couldn't eat. So now I was the same size I was senior year in college. And working all the time meant I couldn't just sit around and stuff my face. Admittedly, I'd been guilty of that during my marriage.

I was glad Carter hadn't seen me when I was a frumpy housewife.

"Thanks." I shrugged as if his compliment didn't mean the world to me. Slowly, I pulled my hands from his and wrapped an arm around Meredith's shoulder and pulled her towards me. She smiled broadly up at me. She was normally a happy kid, but her smile seemed kind of secretive as if she had a secret she was dying to share.

"So what's going on? Why are you waiting outside for me?"

"Today was early dismissal. Teacher's work day," Carter explained.

My eyes widened, and I pulled Meredith closer. "Oh my God, Carter. I'm so sorry. Why didn't you call me? Why didn't anyone call me? I'm so sorry I forgot. I have this new manager at work who's a real ass—"

"Relax," he said gently, again touching my shoulder, and cutting me off from swearing in front of my kid. "I figured there had to be a good reason you weren't here to pick her up and Meredith told me you were working and what time you got off, so it was no problem."

I shook my head. "I feel terrible—"

"Relax. We had fun. And you're only..." He consulted his watch. "Two hours late. That's not too bad."

"Yeah," Meredith piped in, "Danny Schultz's mom is always late. Sometimes I think Danny just sleeps here overnight."

Carter frowned. "Hmm...maybe I should have a talk with Danny's parents."

I laughed. "I'm sure she's exaggerating."

"Nope. I saw his sleeping bag," Meredith said with a sure nod.

"Maybe he was going camping...?"

Meredith gave me a dubious look. "At school? He was going camping at school? I don't think so, Mom."

She had a stubborn look on her face which clearly

meant that I wasn't going to win this argument, so I decided to not even try.

"Thanks for staying with her, Carter, or should I call you Principal Knight since we're on school grounds and all?"

He smiled again, and I found myself again thinking of how much I missed that smile.

"Stop thanking me. It was no problem."

I reached out again to give him a hug and he hugged me back. Gosh, I didn't know how much I'd missed him until the moment I saw him again.

I pulled away. "It's great to see you again. Maybe we'll run into each other again… but you know, not because of a mom failure."

He laughed. "Yeah, that would be nice."

"Bye, Principal K," Meredith said as I took her hand and walked toward the car.

We climbed in and I gave a final wave to Carter who stood there watching us drive away. He waved back and then started toward his car.

I looked back at him and noticed that Meredith was staring at me from the backseat of the car. She still had that silly smile on her face.

"What?" I said. "What's the big secret?"

"Mom?"

"Yeah?"

"Was Principal Knight your boyfriend?"

"What?" I sputtered. "No. We were just friends. You know buddies. Just like you're friends with Danny Schultz."

"I'm not friends with Danny. He just sits next to me at school."

"Okay… well, a long time ago, Carter, umm, Principal Knight and I were really good friends. We went to school together."

"Like elementary school?"

I smiled and shook my head. "No. Just college."

"He's really nice. Was he really nice in college, too?"

I nodded. "He was always a nice guy. The nicest guy, actually."

"Are you guys still friends?"

"I think so. We just fell out of touch—"

"Because you married Daddy?"

I shrugged. Could I really blame my marriage for falling out of touch with friends?

"Sometimes life just takes people in different directions, hon. I got married. Carter went to China or Cambodia. Somewhere. People just fall out of touch when they get older."

"Well, Principal Knight is nice. You should be his friend again." She paused and then her eyes grew large in sudden excitement. "I know! I know!"

"What?"

"You should invite him to Auntie Piper's birthday party."

"Dammit," I mumbled under my breath.

"Mom, don't say bad words." Of course she'd heard me.

"Sorry," I mumbled. I'd completely forgotten about Piper's party. It was this weekend. I didn't have a gift and I didn't have anything to wear. Piper had been working out of the country for the past two years but before then, her birthday parties had always been a huge affair.

"We need to find Piper a gift. I forgot to go shopping. We should—"

I didn't have a chance to finish my sentence because I heard a loud sound that sounded like a gunshot and then, the unmistakable sound of a flat tire.

"Grrreeat," I groaned, doing my best to pull over to the side. Traffic wasn't too heavy, but I wasn't the best driver. In fact, driving sort of scared me and I tried not to do it too often. I thought it had too many unknowns and I was right. A flat tire was definitely proof of that.

I wondered if I had a spare in the trunk. I didn't *think* I had a spare in the trunk. If I did, I didn't put it there. Tom had always taken care of all the car stuff. The car I was driving was about five years old and Tom had been the person to keep it maintained. I'd gotten the car in our divorce.

I crossed my fingers a spare would be in the trunk. And then it dawned on me: I didn't know how to change a tire. I was definitely winning the mother of the year award.

After a lot of swearing under my breath and frustration, I managed to get my car to the shoulder of the road. With a feeling of foreboding, I opened the trunk and looked inside. Nothing. Today was just not my day.

Sighing, I reached for my cell phone. I would have to have it towed. I didn't know how much it would cost, but I was pretty sure it would be more than I could afford.

I placed my hand on my forehead, trying not to get upset in front of Meredith who was watching me with wide eyes.

"I'm going to have to call a tow truck, okay? Just sit tight." I hoped my voice sounded reassuring and confident. I didn't feel very confident.

I was dialing the number to a toll service I saw on one of my neighborhood forums, when suddenly a car pulled up behind us.

I instantly tensed up. All sorts of scenarios ran through my head. None of them good. I'd heard about people killing people on the highways all the time. Okay, maybe they were just urban legends, but all urban legends had to come from somewhere, right? Even an urban legend had a grain of truth.

But then I noticed the person behind the wheel and sighed in relief.

"Flat tire?" asked Carter, stepping out the car and coming towards me.

"Yeah. And no spare."

"Well, that's a problem."

"No kidding."

"Hi again, Principal Knight," Meredith shouted looking at us through the back window. She was having a fun time apparently.

He waved to her and then turned back to me. "I have a spare."

I shook my head. "I'm not taking yours. What if you need it?"

He looked at me with an incredulous expression. "Dana. I think the chances of both of us needing the spare are pretty slim."

"I don't know...."

But he was already heading to his trunk. He quickly got the tools he needed and made his way back to my car.

"Hey, you," he called to Meredith. "This will only take five minutes. Want to time me?"

"Yes!"

"Okay... tell me when to go..."

I gave Meredith my phone. She set the timer and then shouted, "On your mark, get set, ready, go!"

She cheered him on exuberantly as I watched. Carter pushed his sleeves up his forearm, showcasing some very well-developed biceps. When had Carter gotten into weightlifting?

Or maybe he had occupied himself by doing pull-ups in the jungle? I felt ridiculous for the thought, but the image made me giggle.

My face must have mirrored my amusement because he looked up at me and said, "What's with the goofy smile?"

I answered honestly, "I just thought of you doing pull-ups in the jungle and it made me laugh."

"What about changing a tire makes you think that I did pull-ups in the jungle?"

I didn't dare mention that I'd been checking him out. Instead I said, "Well, you did live like Tarzan for a few years. At least that's how Piper made it sound."

My answer caught him off-guard and he let out a bark of laughter.

"Time!" Meredith yelled out, interrupting whatever Carter was going to say next.

"No fair. Your mom distracted me."

Meredith shrugged. "Too bad, so sad."

Carter gave me a pointed look. "Your child is just like you."

I smiled. "Thanks."

"What makes you think that was a compliment?" he

joked, and I playfully punched him in the shoulder. I gave him some room then so that he could finish, and he was done pretty quickly.

I noted how his thighs pressed against his pants. Carter had filled out very nicely. And why couldn't I stop checking out someone who had once been one of my best friends?

I chalked it up to loneliness. That had to be it. And I hadn't had sex in a year, so there was that. Not that I wanted to have sex with Carter. *Sex with Carter. Sex with Carter.* Now I couldn't stop repeating it in my mind. I wanted to tell the little inner monologue in my head to shut up, but it was no use.

Quickly, I just blurted out anything, "Thanks for fixing my tire."

"You're welcome," he said, standing up. And then we stood there awkwardly staring at each other. I felt like I needed to thank him somehow since he'd come to my rescue twice already.

"You keep rescuing me from myself," I said with a smile.

"Someone has to," he quipped. Gosh, he hadn't changed at all. Still funny, still handsome, still... Carter.

"Well, you've been a lifesaver. Maybe you can stop by one evening? I could make you dinner."

"That would be nice." He moved a little closer to me and if I wasn't mistaken, I felt a little flush. What was going on? I wasn't attracted to... no... that was not okay. He was my friend. And Meredith's principal!

"So I'll call you..." my voice trailed off as I reached for my car door.

"You don't have my number."

"Put it in her phone." Meredith offered her hands on either side of her face as she leaned on the window with her head poked out staring at us.

I handed Carter my phone and he entered his details.

"Aren't you going to invite him to Auntie Piper's birthday party?" Meredith asked.

"I'm already going to be there."

"You know Auntie Piper?"

"Yep. Your Auntie Piper and your mom were my best friends in college."

Meredith frowned as if in deep thought and then said with great gravity, "If you had to choose between kissing Mommy and kissing Auntie Piper, who would you choose?"

I know I turned beet red.

Carter let out a loud laugh and gathered his things. "That's quite a question, Meredith. But I have a feeling that neither your auntie or your mom is interested in kissing me."

She shrugged and settled back in her seat with a smug smile. "You never know."

"Okay, I think we're done here. I'm mortified." It

wasn't like Meredith to talk about anyone kissing. She always said that kissing was the grossest thing in the world. I guess she'd changed her mind.

"Don't be. You should hear some of the things kids share with me at school. That was pretty mild."

"Glad you think so," I said, lowering myself into my car. I avoided making eye contact with him and thanked him again profusely.

"My pleasure," he said, heading back in the direction of his car.

Groaning, I looked through my side mirror to ensure no one was coming and made my way back into traffic. I looked back at Meredith and said, "Umm, honey. Can we not make comments about me kissing anyone?"

"I guess," she said reluctantly. "But Mom, if Daddy can kiss Becca, why can't you kiss someone else too? It's a free country. And you better start kissing someone else now before you get too old to kiss anyone. And then you'll just be a sad old lady."

"Sad old lady?" I said in shock. "Where do you get this stuff from?"

She shrugged. "I'm just smart like that."

Smart would not have been the word I'd use. I probably would have used intrusive, but hey, she was only five going on six.

The mention of Becca immediately put me in a bad mood. Becca was the nineteen-year-old that my ex-husband had married. I didn't want to think about Tom kissing her, but Meredith had a point. I wasn't ready to move on but at the very least I needed to start thinking about it. I was young and had a whole lot of life to live. It didn't make sense to waste it being bitter about my divorce.

The sun was setting in front of us. It was officially the end of the day. Tomorrow would be better I told myself. I would make sure of it.

3

"This is going to be the best party ever," Meredith exclaimed as we made our way down the street to Piper's house.

"I think so too. But no skipping in the street. Back on the sidewalk, little lady."

She laughed and crossed back over to the sidewalk. We'd been pretty excited about the party for a while now. Because I worked so much and Meredith sometimes stayed after school to participate in glee club, we rarely got a chance to spend any time together except for the weekends when she wasn't at her dad's.

Meredith had insisted on dressing up even though I'd told her the party was going to be super casual. She wore a tiara, a ballerina skirt, and a sequined blouse. Even her shoes had sequins across the front.

I took her hand as we approached Piper's door.

There was a lot of raucous noise on the other side of the door and I briefly wondered if maybe bringing Meredith hadn't been a good idea.

My reservations quickly disappeared when Piper greeted us at the door, wearing a tiara of her own.

"Nice tiara," she said, high-fiving Meredith who looked at her gleefully before exclaiming, "Happy birthday, Auntie Piper."

Piper scooped her up in a big hug and then grabbed me too, pulling me in tight. "Group hug, group hug," she said, laughing.

Piper hadn't changed since college. She was silly and a complete jokester. Finally, she let us go.

"Oh man, did I miss free hugs?" said a voice right behind her.

It was her cousin, Tabitha. We all called her Tabby. Tabby and Piper looked like twins. They both had short dark brown hair and big blue eyes. I think they even went to the same yoga studio.

I hadn't seen Tabby since my divorce. Strangely, during the divorce, none of Tom's family had picked sides. They had remained neutral. I thought it would be weird to show up tonight with all of Tom's family around, but Piper had insisted that I come. She told me if I didn't come then Tom would think that I was still upset over our divorce. I'd quickly informed Piper that I *was* still upset over the divorce. Piper had then given me a speech about women's empowerment and the importance of raising resilient girls.

Her speech had fallen on deaf ears. I'd only been thinking about how fantastic I looked now, so at least when I happened to see Tom's family there, I wouldn't look like a frumpy sack of sadness.

And plus, Tom wasn't going to be there. Meredith had told me he was going to be out of town. He was taking his new wife on vacation to Hawaii. How nice for them, I'd thought bitterly. I'd then smiled secretly to myself as visions of their plane disappearing in the Bermuda Triangle danced in my head. And then I remembered that Bermuda was in the Caribbean and Hawaii was in the Pacific, so my fantasy of them getting eaten by the Kraken as they traveled to some romantic destination most likely wouldn't happen.

It wasn't until my divorce that I realized how unforgiving and vengeful I could be.

Tabby embraced me and then Meredith. "It's so good to see you guys. How's everything going?" She looked a little uncomfortable with the question, but I wasn't. I had an answer prepared that I'd rehearsed lots of times to save face.

"Great! Enjoying my freedom!" I hoped I sounded convincing.

Tabby looked relieved. "Being married really is a

drain. Trust me, that's why I divorced my husband ages ago."

I gave Tabby a pointed look and shot my eyes toward Meredith. Tabby looked clueless for a second and then quickly said. "I mean, your Prince Charming is out there, honey. Just don't marry a frog like your father."

"Jesus, Tabby," Piper said.

"What? What did I say?"

And then seeing Meredith's confused expression, Tabby quickly backtracked. "I love frogs. They're just all green and slimy. Good for dissecting."

"You know what? I think we're going to get some cake," Piper said, coming to the rescue. "Doesn't cake sound delicious, Meredith?"

She nodded, and I took her hand. I shook my head at Tabby as I walked by and she mouthed, "I'm sorry."

Same ol' Tabby, I thought to myself. She had verbal diarrhea. Sweetest woman, but she didn't know when to just be quiet.

And now I'd have to have a mother-daughter talk with Meredith defending her father who was the last guy I wanted to defend right now. Gosh, maybe I should have just stayed home.

"So, hon. Just ignore your cousin Tabby. Sometimes she says things that she shouldn't say."

"Just like Danny Schultz."

"Huh?"

"Danny always talks about gross things, so Ms. Weatherly makes him apologize or takes away one of his stars."

I nodded, glad that she at least understood the point I was trying to make. "Well, yeah. Like that. Except that Tabby is an adult so we can't put her in time out."

Meredith giggled. "That would be funny. I've never seen an adult in time out before."

"Well, if Aunt Tabby continues saying things that she shouldn't say, that's exactly what's going to happen to her."

Meredith giggled some more and then Tabby popped up again. She looked relieved that we were laughing.

"So have I been forgiven?" she asked Meredith.

Meredith nodded. "But be nice or you'll have an adult time out."

Tabby laughed, looked unsure and then said to me, "Oh man, she's serious, isn't she?"

"Like a heart attack," I said reaching for a slice of cake and handing it to Meredith. "She's one tough cookie."

Meredith greedily took the cake out of my hand, helped herself to a big bite and then said with a mouthful, "I am one tough cookie, but I loooooooovvve cake."

Tabby couldn't help but smile. "Yeah, you're a tough one. Just like your mom. Hey, how about after you finish your cake I'll take you out back to see your other cousins? They're about to watch a magician."

Meredith immediately stopped talking and her eyes went wide. "Magic? Like a real live magic show? Like in Vegas?"

"Where'd you hear about Vegas?" Tabby asked incredulously.

"Becca talks about it all the time. It's like her favorite place. She said she'll take me there when I turn sixteen."

My eyes widened, and I was a second away from losing it, when I guess Tabby noticed and cut in.

"Las Vegas is for older people. You can go when you're twenty-one."

"But Becca goes all the time..."

"Well, Becca is just a special kind of person," I heard Tabby say as she led Meredith away.

I was so busy standing there seething that I didn't notice when someone joined me. It was Piper.

"You okay? You're frowning. Since when does cake make anyone frown? It's a happy food."

I shook my head. "Apparently, Becca told Meredith that she'll take her to Vegas when she's sixteen."

Piper laughed. "Are you kidding me?"

"Yes, I'm serious." My voice grew deep as I became even more upset.

Piper noticed and said, "You look like you're about to

explode. Take it easy. You have about ten years until then and by then, Becca will be older and wiser—"

"We can only hope," I growled.

Piper laughed again and said, "Okay, maybe not wiser, but I'm sure she meant that she would take her to shows and fun family-friendly things. I doubt she planned to take her to a male all-nude revue and then out for nonstop drinks."

"I don't know Becca, but just from what I hear about her, I sort of feel that's probably something she would definitely do."

Piper considered her next words carefully. "Becca is pretty much an airhead but she's really good with Meredith."

"And how would you know that?" My question came off as accusatory. Was my best friend hanging out with my enemy?

Piper looked guilty before saying, "We went to the spa together when I got back into town."

I knew it was stupid, but I felt betrayed. Not only was Becca now married to my ex, but apparently she was also hanging out with my best friend. I didn't even have time to spend time with my best friend. How dare she.

"She has some nerve spending time with you," I growled. "And I can't believe you let her spend time with you! What were you thinking? Whose side are you on?"

Piper held up her hands, as if trying to defend herself from my verbal assault. "I'm on your side. Always have been. I never wanted you to date Tom. Remember?"

She was right. When Tom would run into Piper on campus, she went out of her way to ignore him. They weren't exactly close. She said that he was a jerk to her growing up and still a jerk now. I'd refused to believe her. He'd been so cute and so mature.

I didn't start dating him until about six months after we'd met, and I remember Piper saying, "Oh well, I tried to warn you. He's a douchebag. You'll see."

I'd ignored her warnings. Tom and I did the long-distance thing for a few years after he graduated and once I'd graduated we'd moved in together and gotten married shortly after that. I'd thought Piper would have been thrilled that we were no longer just best friends, but also sisters.

But no. She had said, "Oh well, you've done it now," when I'd showed her my engagement ring.

I remembered getting upset with her and not speaking to her for a few days. But then Carter had told me that I was being silly... that Piper had never been a fan of her brother so it shouldn't be a surprise that she wasn't ecstatic that I was marrying him.

Carter had been right, of course, and come to think of it, he had helped resolve every squabble I'd had with Piper over the years.

"Deep in thought, I see. If you're trying to decide between the chocolate cake and the plain vanilla, just go with the chocolate."

Speak of the devil... I smiled as I turned toward Carter.

"Hi, you look..." my voice trailed off. "Great. Very clean." Very clean? Did I just tell Carter that he looked clean? What was wrong with me? Had getting a divorce also lowered my IQ?

Carter laughed and said, "Thanks, I think. You look very clean too." He took a moment to study my figure and I couldn't help myself. I did a little turn. I was wearing a stunning red bodycon dress that I couldn't fit into a year ago. It had been a birthday gift from my mom who had a fantastic sense of fashion. Unfortunately, at the time she'd bought it three sizes too small. I'm pretty sure it was her passive-aggressive way of telling me to lose weight.

Well, my divorce had accomplished what dieting and exercising probably wouldn't have. I was down four sizes and had gotten my mom to take the dress in a little. She'd been ecstatic.

"Being fat didn't suit you," she had chirped happily.

My mom could be as blunt as she could be passive aggressive. Dad, of course, had also chimed in. It's like he'd waited until I was an adult to have an opinion about everything I did.

"She's right you know. No one wants a wife with a double chin. You can't find a husband that way."

"Who says I'm looking for another husband?" I'd regretted stopping by then. I should have just eaten oatmeal for dinner every night for a week to afford an actual tailor.

Dad had replied, "Women need men. You're no different. You'll look for another husband soon enough."

Mom had looked at dad and then at me and said deadpan, "Women need men like I need a hole in the head."

We'd shared a smile. That was probably the only thing my mom and I had shared in my entire adult life.

I turned my attention back to the present and with it, to Carter who started clapping slowly.

"That is a very sexy dress."

"Thank you," I said, feeling like a billion dollars. I was pretty plain with unremarkable brown hair and unre-markable brown eyes. I was average height and kind of just average all around, so it was nice to feel beautiful. I hadn't felt that way in a long time.

Feeling good, I chatted with Carter. We helped ourselves to some cake and were about to take a seat when the doorbell rang.

I didn't see Piper and all the other guests that were near the door ignored it, so I made my way to it.

I opened it, saw who was standing there, and closed it back forcefully and then I walked away.

Carter was apparently the only one who noticed, and he looked at me funny as I plastered a smile on my face, grabbed my slice of cake and sat down next to him.

"Who was at the door?"

"Nobody."

"You sure, because I thought for sure I saw—"

And then the doorbell rang again. This time one of Piper's friends went to answer it. I frowned. *Now* someone wanted to answer the door. Great.

"So Carter, tell me about what's going with you? Are you seeing someone?"

"Well, actually..." he started talking but I wasn't listening. I was too tense and busy listening for the two people I'd slammed the door on.

"Tom's here," Carter said suddenly stopping his story that I hadn't even been paying attention to. He was looking past my shoulder, just to the right of me.

"No freaking kidding," I mumbled, sinking down in my chair as if that would help make me invisible.

"And he's brought someone?" Carter said rising a little bit out of his chair to be nosy.

"His new wife," I growled.

"Wife? She's just a child." Carter's voice was incredulous.

"She's nineteen."

Carter grimaced. "Tell me she's not also his secretary? I always thought Tom was a walking cliché, but even that would be too formulaic for him, I would hope."

"Meredith said they met in the grocery store."

"Really?" Carter said sitting back and looking away from Tom and Becca. He was smiling now. "Did they bond over feta? Did he sweet talk her in an aisle surrounded by sausage and bacon?"

I found myself smiling as well. And then my smile faded when I heard Tabby say, "Dude, your ex-wife is here. You're not supposed to be here."

Tabby didn't know how to whisper. She also didn't know how to be discreet. My shoulders tensed as the whole room turned around to look at me. Okay, maybe it wasn't the whole room, but it felt like it.

I'd never met Becca in person. She had been dating Tom for a few months before he married her, but in that time I hadn't once met her. Tom had been careful to arrange that she didn't show up at any of the pickups. I liked to think that I wouldn't act out if she had, but right after Tom and I separated before our divorce I'd been a bitter, resentful person. I'd blamed Becca for our failed marriage.

Tom swore that they hadn't been having an affair, and I wanted to believe him, but I didn't know if that made me naive.

My shoulders were tense. My mouth was dry. I didn't know how to feel, but I hated that this was all so public.

Just when I was thinking about making my way to the back door to escape the situation instead of facing it, an arm slid around my shoulders. I looked up at Carter in surprise.

"I thought you could use some support," he said simply.

"Thanks, Carter," I looked up at him and smiled. It was nice to have my other best friend back.

"Good evening, Carter. Hello, Dana," Tom said standing there looking dispassionate. He was expressionless as he looked between me and Carter, but I knew Tom well. I knew a dispassionate look meant displeasure.

There had always been bad blood between Tom and Carter. I never understood why. I guessed it was because they were polar opposites. Carter worried about saving the world while Tom just wanted to buy it. Carter was about substance and leading a meaningful life. Tom just wanted to be entertained by life and it was his motto to work hard and play hard.

As I looked at the woman to his right, I realized that he probably played too hard.

"Dana," Tom said resignedly, as if he never wanted

this moment to happen. "This is Becca. Becca this is Dana."

Becca wasn't what I expected. Yes, she was skinny, and she looked very young, but instead of looking like a ditzy blonde, she looked like a cartoon character. She had super curly, unruly blonde hair and large blue eyes. She looked like she should have been a Disney princess. No wonder Meredith liked her so much.

She studied me as I studied her, and she was the first to reach her hand out.

"It's nice to meet you, Dana."

Oh, she was polite. I didn't like that. Now I didn't have a reason to hate her. I wanted her to be a jerk so that I could continue to feel like a woman scorned.

"Is this your boyfriend?" she asked with a hopeful tone to her voice.

I looked around, wondering who she was talking about. And then I remembered that Carter still had his arm wrapped around my shoulder.

"Carter's just a friend of the family," Tom answered for me, giving Carter a long look.

"Actually, I'm a friend of Dana's," Carter corrected Tom, not missing a beat.

Becca's look went from hopeful to pity. Damn it, she felt sorry for me. For some reason, that made me angry.

"Carter, don't be coy," I said flirtatiously, wrapping an arm around his waist.

He gave me a funny look but didn't pull away. I lowered my voice and said in a stage whisper, "I didn't want to say anything, but Carter and I are dating."

Tom looked like he had been slapped. "What?"

Carter removed his arm from my shoulder and instead pulled me close to him around the waist.

Without missing a beat, he said, "Now you want to be open about it, hon? I was sort of enjoying it being just our little secret. But since it's not a secret anymore..." he let his voice trail off as he tucked a hair behind my ear, touching my face in the process and sending an unexpected shiver down my spine.

He tilted my face up and with confusion in my eyes, he leaned down and kissed me softly on the lips. I couldn't remember the last time I'd been kissed, but I knew I didn't want it to end. I felt suddenly like a heroine in a storybook, a fairy tale where I was winning in life instead of feeling like a loser.

Suddenly, Carter was pulling away and I opened my eyes, having not even realized that I'd closed them. And apparently, I'd also wrapped my arms around his neck.

He smiled down at me. His eyes teasing and self-satisfied. I couldn't help but smile back and then I noticed the audience around us, and I self-consciously pulled away.

I turned to meet Tom's eyes. He looked away uncomfortably.

Becca, on the other hand, had a completely different reaction. "Oh my gosh, I knew it. I just knew it. You guys were too cute together to not be a couple. And you guys make a cuuuute couple." She gleefully clapped her hands together.

No wonder Becca and Meredith got along. It was almost as if they were the same age.

Before I could say anything, Tom was pulling Becca away, mumbling something about, "Giving the lovebirds some space."

I could hear the sarcasm dripping from each word.

The audience we had suddenly turned away and pretended to be looking elsewhere. Tom and Becca made their way outside and I watched them disappear.

When they were gone, I looked back at Carter and slowly pulled myself from his embrace. I instantly missed his warmth and shook my head at the thought. Carter was my friend. A friend whose lips had been pressed against mine a minute ago, but my friend none-theless.

"Stop looking so self-satisfied," I said to him softly so that no one would overhear us.

He smiled wider. "You should have seen the look on your face after I kissed you."

Great, he was going to tease me about it.

"Shut up, Carter."

"I tried to break the kiss after the first like second,

but you had your arms wrapped around me like a bear trap—"

"Shut up, Carter."

"Your arms were like a vice. I imagine that's what it would feel like to be hugged by a python."

"If you don't shut up I'll strangle you with a python."

He laughed then, tossing his head back and I couldn't help but laugh with him. Suddenly, the tension I felt at our very intimate exchange evaporated.

He was clearly just a friend trying to save my butt from humiliation.

"This is the part where you thank me for coming to your rescue," he said sitting back and resting his hands behind his head.

"What? I'm not thanking you for slobbering on me. Whatever."

He sat up, "Slobbering? Woman, that was the best kiss you've ever had."

Now it was my turn to laugh. "I don't know... it sort of felt like being licked by a puppy."

He mockingly grabbed at his heart. "You're so cruel. Just so cruel."

I smiled wickedly. "I try my best."

Before we could continue teasing each other, Meredith came running over.

"Mommy, Mommy, did you see Daddy and Becca?"

"Sure did, sweetie," I said with forced cheer.

"Isn't Becca nice?" she asked climbing into my lap and loping an arm around my neck.

I swallowed back the not so nice things I wanted to say and instead said, "Yep."

"And pretty?"

"Yep."

"Just as pretty as you, Mommy," Meredith said giving me a sweet smile. My daughter was an angel. I didn't deserve her.

"You're the best kid in the whole world, you know that?" I said, giving her a hug.

She laughed. "You always say that."

"That's because it's true."

"I second that," Carter said.

Meredith gave him a look that clearly said she didn't believe him. "Mr. Carter you say that to all the kids."

"What can I say? I'm surrounded by amazing children."

"Danny Schultz isn't all that amazing," she said with a frown.

"What is with you and Danny Schultz?" I asked. She always seemed to find a way to work him into the conversation.

She shrugged. "I don't know. He just bugs me."

And with that, she hopped off my lap and went looking for cake.

I turned back to Carter and said, "Kids. They have a

mind of their own."

"They sure do."

Whatever else Carter was about to say was soon overshadowed by the bass suddenly blasting from the speakers.

We'd gone from 80s pop to 90s pop. Fun, but not really because I couldn't really dance to this type of music. And from what I remembered, neither could Carter. Yet, that didn't stop him from grabbing me by the hand and pulling me towards the dance floor which was Piper's living room.

Piper was already there, shaking it. Meredith was on the dance floor too, chocolate cake on her hands, being spun around and around by Becca who I hadn't even noticed had reappeared.

Tom was nowhere to be found, but he wasn't a dancer. He avoided the dancefloor like the plague.

I pulled my hand away from Carter and shook my head. He gave me a sad look and mouthed, "Come on."

I shook my head no and shouted so that he could hear me, "I can't dance."

"Neither can I," he yelled back, and then he whispered loudly in my ear, "But I'm your fake boyfriend, remember? You can't leave me hanging."

He had a point. He extended his hand again and raised his brows and wiggled them at me. He was so silly. I giggled, feeling as if we were in college again.

"Come on, you know you want to."

Shrugging, I let him take my hand and together we made our way to the dance floor. We did a weird two-step and a lot of punching the air. Meredith watched us, running into us every now and again. The magician—meant to be entertaining the kids—was also on the dance floor, tossing fake handkerchiefs at people while bouncing around.

A few kids joined him and suddenly it felt more like a mosh pit instead of a house party. At one point, a little kid ran right into my butt, sending me flying towards Carter.

He caught me easily and said with another stupid grin, "You just can't resist me, can you?"

"You're ridiculous," I said, but I didn't pull away as he wrapped his arms around me and just held me as we rocked back and forth to the music that had slowed in tempo just a little.

Companionship was something I hadn't really had with Tom, I thought, as Carter held me. And I hadn't made any friends while being married to Tom. It had been a lonely existence, I realized now. If it hadn't been for Meredith I probably would have been depressed. But thinking back, I had been depressed.

I was an emotional eater and had a tendency to eat my way to feeling good. That probably explained the extra forty pounds I'd gained while married. I realized that I'd lost part of myself when I'd been married, the part of me that had been a great friend.

Carter and I had been so close in college. He and Piper had meant the world to me and I'd let my marriage to Tom change that relationship. I'd let my marriage to Tom change me.

I rested my head against Carter's chest and thought of how good it felt to be there. As usual, Carter had come to my rescue. And after struggling to make it on my own, it kind of felt good to have someone come to my rescue.

The song stopped, and I reluctantly raised my head. I'd expected to look up at Carter and see the same teasing look he had given me earlier, but no. This time the look he gave me was something else, something I couldn't identify.

But it was gone quickly, and he reached for my hand which I gladly let him take. There was tension now between us that hadn't been there before.

I didn't know what to say or how to ease it, so I tried a lame joke, "You're still the worst dancer in the room."

He laughed lightly, but he looked lost in thought. "Not much has changed over the years…"

"I don't know. You've changed."

He looked pensive. "You think so?"

"Yeah," I said suddenly feeling a little shy around him. I didn't understand why. I noticed then that we'd migrated towards the buffet table and he was still holding my hand.

I pulled away and he looked down and said, "Oh, sorry."

"Are you crushing on my hand or something?" I teased.

"Or something..." he said softly. His voice was gentle and his words simple but packed with meaning.

I didn't know what to say or how to respond, so I said nothing and reached for a cup of punch. I hoped the punch was spiked. My emotions were everywhere, and I didn't know what to do about them besides ignore them or deny that I found myself attracted to one of my best friends.

I chugged back the punch and was disappointed that there was no liquor in it at all.

I felt Carter's hand on my shoulder and slowly turned back to face him.

"Dana, can we talk?"

"What is going on with you guys? I heard you two made out in front of my brother and his new child bride?" said Piper, popping up from seemingly nowhere.

"What? No, no, no, that's not what happened," I quickly started to explain. "Your brother popped up with the new missus and Carter saved me by—"

"Sticking his tongue in your mouth?" Piper asked with a laugh.

I blushed, and Carter again came to my rescue, "No tongue… but I was tempted."

I covered my eyes with my hands like a little girl and groaned. "You guys are killing me. Please stop."

I felt Carter pulling my hands off my face and he was smiling at me. He gave me a wink and then turned to Piper and said, "Becca asked if Dana and I were an item, so we faked a kiss so that Dana wouldn't seem like a bitter divorcee with no prospects for a future."

"Wow, thanks for that, Carter," I said, planting my hands on my hips. "Way to make me sound desperate."

He shrugged. "You're welcome."

"I figured as much," Piper said, and then gave me a regretful look. "I'm sorry Tom showed up."

"You don't have to apologize for inviting your brother."

"That's just it. I didn't invite him. He invited himself."

"Oh, really?"

"Really. Ever since he married Becca, he's trying to act like brother of the year."

"That's weird."

"Tell me about it. I think it's Becca's influence. She's from a big family, but they live out in Oregon so she never sees them. I think she's kind of lonely. I think besides Tom, the only family she has here is her dad."

"Being married to Tom was a lonely experience," I said, suddenly feeling sorry for her. She hadn't known what she was marrying into apparently. "I was determined to hate her but I guess she's not that bad, and Meredith adores her."

"She's actually a really sweet girl."

"Girl being the operative word," Carter said dryly.

"She is super young."

"Well, you married Tom at twenty-one, so it really isn't that big of an age difference," Piper added.

"You're right." Tom had married another doe-eyed hopeful. Typical.

I wasn't ready to keep singing Becca's praises, after all, she was my replacement. She might be lonely, but she was living a life of luxury, while I was just busy trying to stay afloat. She was living my old life and that still made me feel a little jealous. I hadn't reached the point yet where I was nonchalant about my divorce. The pain was still there. Still raw. I'd had my life snatched away from me and now someone else was enjoying it. Well, kind of enjoying it.

I didn't want to think about my ex anymore, so instead, I changed the subject. "Where have you been, birthday girl? This is your party but I haven't seen you since you let us in."

She sighed heavily and leaned against the buffet table with a faraway look in her eyes, "I've been trying to get the magician's number."

I frowned. "Why? Do you owe him money or something? Don't you normally have to pay for those types of freelancing services upfront?"

"Not his business number, silly. I already have that. His personal number."

"You're interested in the magician?" Carter said, unable to keep the incredulity out of his voice. I'm not sure why he was so surprised. Piper had a way of dating outcasts, weirdos, non-conformists, and hippies. They were her favorite.

"So how many magicians have you dated in the past? Four? Five?" I asked.

"I wish," she said with a wistful look. "Not one. I was on this website for people who live off gigs. So there I was looking for caterers when boom, the site suggests that a magician would be the perfect party favor. So I clicked on it—"

Carter snorted. "Of course."

"Shut up," Piper joked before continuing. "Anyway, like I was saying, I clicked on the ad and this gorgeous man wearing a magician suit pops up on my screen. And not only was he cute, but crazy inexpensive." She leaned forward and motioned for us to do the same. "You guys, I think I might be in love. When he arrived, he did this magic trick where he found a bouquet of roses behind my ear. Is that not the sweetest thing you've ever heard of?"

"He's a magician. That's what they do. They pull

things from behind your ear," Carter said, not sounding impressed.

"Yeah, coins and stuff, but these were roses. Fresh roses." She looked from me to Carter. "Come on, you guys, it means something."

"Yeah, it means that he probably lost his bouquet of fake roses," I said dryly.

Piper rolled her eyes, grabbed a pretzel from the table and tossed it into her mouth. She wasn't even done chewing as she said to us. "You two suck. Like a lot. I need new friends."

"You love us," Carter said, also helping himself to pretzels.

She grinned. "You're right. And I've missed you guys. It's so good to be home. And it's so great that we're all here together. We haven't all lived in one place since college."

Piper had joined the Peace Corps right after college. She had served in Bolivia and then made her way around Latin America for five years, working with various nonprofits and NGOs. Now she was running a very profitable translation services business online, so she had finally decided to come back home.

It's funny that both my closest friends had traveled the world and lived in different countries, leading exciting lives, while I hadn't even held a job in nearly a decade.

Suddenly, I didn't feel so hot. And then I felt ridiculous. They were my friends. And it had been me who had let that friendship falter. Piper had invited me to join her on a trip or to visit her countless times, even before Meredith had been born. I'd declined them all. And then afterward, when she and Carter would meet up somewhere in a foreign country, they always tried to convince me to come visit and I never did.

I understood that life sometimes happens. Sometimes friends fall out of touch. But we hadn't fallen out of touch. I hadn't prioritized my friendships and had been lonely as a result.

"You know, we should all get together for lunch."

"Tacos Tuesday like we used to do?" Carter asked with a smile.

I was about to groan and mention that salsa gave me bad heartburn now, but I didn't want to sound like the old lady I felt I was.

"You're on," I said. "You in, Piper?"

"Yep."

The magician appeared not so magically next to us.

"My time's up but I don't mind sticking around."

"Off the clock?" Piper asked flirtatiously.

"Anything for you, birthday girl," he said with a charming smile.

I looked at Carter and he looked at me. The other

two were too into each other to notice as we slithered away.

"Well, he seems nice."

Carter shrugged. "Better than her falling for a clown."

"Agreed."

The noise level of the party had increased to a kind of deafening roar.

"I think I need a little air," I shouted to Carter.

"Me too," he said, tucking my elbow in his and leading the way.

I didn't know Piper knew so many people. There were at least thirty people there now and only a few faces I recognized. I shouldn't have been surprised because, as they say, Piper never met a stranger.

We made our way to a little bench in her front yard and I sat down. Carter stayed standing and leaned against a tree.

Surreptitiously, I looked at him. I remembered back in college how I would be stressed out about exams and he would take me to go get a burger and watch some wacky foreign film. And I thought about how he always let me hang out with him and his parents whenever family day happened on campus.

My parents had always been too busy to show up. And the one time that they did show, they spent most of their time criticizing me for some imaginary slight.

Carter's parents had been the exact opposite of mine. His parents, although divorced, were a unified front. They were super supportive, and both had remarried so their partners were also pretty great. For family day at school, Carter never had to worry about who wouldn't show up. Both sets of parents with their new spouses always did. I joked with Carter that his two sets of parents seemed more like polygamists than anything else since they all got along so well.

Carter had said it had taken years for them to reach that point. I'd marveled at them, not knowing that years later I would be struggling to do the same. I wasn't at the point yet where I could happily hang out with Becca and Tom and not let it bother me.

Just thinking about co-parenting made me exhausted. I stretched and let out a big yawn. Suddenly, I was tired.

"Getting tired?"

I shrugged self-consciously. "Yeah, kind of." Who was I kidding? I could barely keep my eyes open. It was time to go.

"I think I've had enough partying for one night. I should go find Meredith."

My shoulders were tense again. I rolled them and reached a hand around to rub one side that was full of tension.

Carter stood up from the tree he had been leaning

against and came and sat next to me on the tiny bench.

"Turn around," Carter ordered.

I did as he said and sighed when his warm hands massaged my shoulders. "That feels great," I sighed.

All the tension from my shoulders melted and I leaned against Carter, my back against his chest. He smelled yummy. I wondered why I didn't notice before. I wondered if it was cologne or some sort of scrub that his wacky mom had given him. I knew she ran a shop on Etsy selling all sorts of all natural, organic goodies.

He stopped rubbing my shoulders and then started stroking my arms. His touch gave me goosebumps and felt kind of familiar, intimate even.

"What are you doing, Carter?" I asked softly, not moving, but feeling I needed to say something before things progressed further.

"Warming you up," he said, his mouth close to my ear. "You have goosebumps."

I shivered then a little but not because I was cold.

"Carter—" I started, turning to face him.

"Hey, Mom. There you are," Meredith said, appearing on the front porch with Tom and Becca at her side.

I instantly sat up, pulling myself away from Carter's embrace as they approached. And then I remembered that I was supposed to be Carter's girlfriend. But I also didn't want Meredith to think Carter and I were an item.

Confused, I just sat there, trying to figure out what to do next. Carter made it easy for me by letting go of me and standing up. He took my hand and helped me up too.

Meredith grinned when she saw us together, "I knew you liked my mommy," she said, giving Carter a wide smile. Hmmm... I guess I didn't have to worry about her reaction.

Tom again looked at us as if he wanted to punch Carter in the face. Jealous much? I thought to myself with a self-satisfied inner grin.

"Do you think it would be okay if Meredith spent the night?" Becca said. "I know we normally get her on Wednesdays, but since it's spring break and all, do you think maybe I could take her to go pick strawberries with me? My mom and I used to do it when I was a kid, so I thought she might like to go too."

I wanted to say, "Aren't you still a kid?"

But instead, I looked at Meredith who had her hands folded together as if she were begging while she beseeched me with her eyes saying, "Please...please...please."

"Sure," I said, "Who can resist a face like that? But what about a change of clothes..."

Becca waved her hand in reassurance. "Oh, she has a full wardrobe at our house. With lots of tiaras, I made sure of that."

She took Meredith's hand and the two looked at each other like they were best of friends. And that's when it hit me. I didn't need to be worried about Becca and Meredith's relationship. It was totally different from the relationship I had with Meredith. It was almost as if they were sisters, strangely enough.

I mean, hey, they were close enough in age to be related.

I bent down and kissed Meredith on the head and she hugged me tightly. "Have fun, sweetheart. I'll pick you up tomorrow evening. Sound good?"

"That sounds great, Mom. I'll save you some strawberries."

"Please do," I said straightening up.

Tom didn't say a word during the whole exchange, which was fine with me. The less I had to talk to him, the better. In fact, I figured maybe I would just contact Becca instead when I needed to discuss anything that had to do with Meredith. It would stop me from being a jerk to him if I just didn't have to talk to him.

Maybe I would eventually get to the point that Carter's parents had. Except I didn't have anyone, but Tom did. I wondered if that would change any time soon.

"Bye, Mommy. Have a good night. Bye, Principal K."

"Principal K?" Tom asked.

"Carter's the new principal at Meredith's school.

They sent out a notice."

"Hmm..." was all Tom said before turning away from us. "Let's go, hon," he said, and I didn't know which lady he was talking to, but Becca waved good-bye to us happily and took Meredith by the hand.

They skipped away together, laughing as if they were best of friends.

"They're like sisters," Carter said, reading my mind.

"Yeah."

"I guess that's a good thing," he said with uncertainty in his voice.

I shrugged. "I don't know. This whole co-parenting thing is new to me."

"Considering that you divorced recently, you're doing a pretty good job."

"Really? You think so?"

"Well, you're not shouting at each other in public or repeatedly taking each other to court, so yeah."

I winced. "Sorry. I guess you experienced a lot of that."

He shook his head. "Luckily, they stopped being bitter and angry long enough to realize they were doing more harm than good."

"How are your parents, by the way?"

"Great. They're happy I'm home. Now they get to guilt me into celebrating every major holiday with them."

I laughed. "You're lucky they love you."

He shrugged. "I'm glad to have them. It's great being home. I've missed them. I've missed Piper, and of course I've missed you."

"I missed you, too."

We stared at each other and I couldn't help but recall a night around eight years ago that I knew at that very moment he was also thinking about. It was a night that neither of us had apparently forgotten or talked about.

"I'm going to head in and tell Piper that I'm leaving." My voice sounded breathless, but I couldn't help it. Emotions I'd buried a long time ago were starting to surface and I needed space to process them.

It seemed he did too. He moved out of my way and said, "Yeah. I think I'll head home now. Tell Piper I'll catch up with her later."

"Will do," I said as he turned and walked away without another word.

I stood there and just watched him walk away. Watching Carter walk away was something that I was accustomed to doing.

I shook my head. Who would have thought that such a fun night would bring up ghosts from our past?

With that thought, I opened the door and walked back into Piper's house, determined to not think about the night years ago when I almost lost one of my best friends.

4

"**$\mathcal{M}$om**, Mom. This one is so funny. What do you call a cow on the ground?"

I shrugged as I turned the wheel of the car. "I don't know. What do you call it?"

"Come on, Mom. Try to guess. Come on." I'd given Meredith a riddle and joke book for her birthday a few months ago and she thoroughly enjoyed reading a joke or two to me each morning while driving her to school.

"Okay, okay. Ummm, a sleeping cow?"

She laughed hard. Deep belly laughs that shook her whole body. Her laughter was contagious, and I started smiling too.

"Nooo," she said in between giggles. "Ground beef. That's the answer."

"Ground beef?" I said, smiling. "Now that's a good one."

"Yep," she said contently.

She had come home with a ton of strawberries after her trip with Becca. I knew we'd be having strawberries covered in whipped cream for dessert. Either that or we'd be having lots of smoothies.

I pulled into the drop-off line and she scampered out, running quickly to catch up with friends.

"I love you, pumpkin," I called to her.

She kept on running and then abruptly turned around, blew me a kiss, and went running again up the school steps.

"That's my angel," I said softly.

I was about to pull away when I saw Carter chatting with a group of ladies. They started laughing at something he'd said and I knew instantly that the new principal was getting some very special attention.

I wasn't paying attention and didn't realize the van in front of me wasn't going anywhere. To my chagrin, I went into it as I tried to pull away.

There was a loud bang and then a screeching sound as I attempted to dislodge the license plate from the van's rear.

I gave up and prepared to be mortified and yelled at —the story of my life.

Ten seconds later, that's exactly what happened. "What the hell? What in the holy hell? Did you not see me sitting there? What the hell?" the furious mom said as she stared at the damage I'd caused.

"It's not too bad," I said, once I summoned the courage to get out the car and look at it.

Her eyes widened, and I swore she was going to hit me at any moment. "Not too bad? Not too bad! There are scratches all over the back of my car. And look at my license plate. It looks like it was attacked by the Cookie Monster."

I let out a nervous giggle. Cookie Monster? From Sesame Street? You could tell she had a young child.

"So you think this is funny?" She balled up her fists and I tried not to run away. "You suck, you know that, right? Thank you for screwing up my day. Now my insurance rates will go up and then how am I going to afford this fancy private school?"

I opened my mouth and then closed it. I didn't know what to say.

"Forget it. You don't understand." She looked at my car and then said with derision, "If that vehicle of yours is any indication, you're either the nanny or your kid is here on scholarship, so what do you care about tuition?"

Hold on. What was she trying to say? Was she calling me poor?

I narrowed my eyes, "Just because I don't drive a stupid Range Rover doesn't mean I have to take abuse from you."

"Abuse? I'll show you abuse!"

She stepped up and her face was only inches from mine. I'd never been in a fight before. I didn't know how to throw a punch, but I figured I could just tackle her to the ground and bite her. Sort of like what toddlers did at the playground.

Before I had the opportunity to try my toddler style karate, Carter grabbed me by the sweater and pulled me away. He stepped in between us and said, "Ladies, how about we calm it down a little, stop exchanging insults, and not make a scene in front of the children."

"She started it," I yelled like an elementary schooler.

"What? Bitch. You hit my car!"

My mouth fell open and I pointed at her and then looked at Carter, "She said the B word."

"Wow, you're real mature."

"Ladies, let's go, inside. My office. Now."

He didn't wait for us to follow. He just turned around and marched toward the office. Feeling terrible, I sheepishly followed behind him.

The other parent wasn't sheepish at all. She huffily stalked past me, hitting me in my shoulder as she followed behind Carter.

"Hey," I said. "Watch it."

"Watch it? From someone who bumped my car?"

"Bumped exactly. It was just a bump."

She growled at me. Literally growled at me and I jumped back.

"Ladies, please. My office, stat," Carter ordered as he opened the door and stood there waiting for us to walk past him.

The other mom went past me. And I sheepishly walked past Carter, but not before he shot me a little smile.

I guess I wasn't in trouble, after all. Carter would protect me… if the other mom didn't find a way to kill me first. Twenty minutes later, the other mom left the office in a better mood. Carter had really put on the charms and the other mom had not only apologized to me for calling me poor, but she had also been really patient while I looked for my insurance information.

"You know, you need to stop coming to my rescue."

"Then stop getting in trouble."

I looked around. "I'm in the principal's office again. Apparently, I can't stay out of trouble."

"You've always had a penchant for getting into trouble. Remember that time you and Piper went streaking across campus and got locked out of your dorm?"

A startled laugh burst from my lips. "My nether regions were freezing."

He smiled and said, "It was fifty degrees outside. You two were crazy."

"Yep. We were."

I wanted to stay there reminiscing about the old days, but I knew I had to go. "I guess I'll leave. I know you have work to do."

He nodded. "Plenty."

"It's weird seeing you look so official. I never pictured you as a principal."

He laughed. "It isn't what I pictured either, but I don't know. It fits."

"You look good behind there."

"Thanks," he said, standing up. "Try not to bump into anyone else, okay?"

I sighed. "I'll do my best but I can't make any promises."

His administrative assistant knocked on his door and then poked her head in. "Your meeting with the board is in five minutes." Just as quickly as she interrupted, she disappeared.

"Let me get out of your way."

"You're never in the way,"

I looked away, suddenly uncomfortable and made my way out of the office, "Don't forget tonight's play," he called to me.

"Oh, crap, I'd already totally forgotten. I'm a terrible mom."

"Nope. Just a busy one. I only remembered because Becca called the school this morning to confirm. Like bright and early this morning."

I couldn't help it. I was annoyed. I already had to share my daughter with Becca every other weekend courtesy of our custody order. And she spent one day a week over at their home, as well. And now Becca planned to attend school events? Great.

I wish I could be the better person and not be bothered by the fact that my ex had married so quickly, but this time last year I'd been married. It was a whirlwind of events and my emotions were everywhere.

THE NEXT DAY as I made my way to work, I was still feeling out of sorts. I felt like I was living my life on auto-pilot. I totally didn't feel like going to work, but I had to do what I had to do. That's what Tom's grandmother used to say. She was a sweet lady and had come a couple of times to campus to visit Tom and Piper.

As soon as I pulled up in front of Primrose, I saw Lucy outside taking a smoke break.

"Hey, you," I said, and she gave me a little smile. Normally, Lucy was a chatterbox. Immediately, I knew something was up.

"You okay?" I asked.

She sighed. "Our new boss is being an ass."

With a sigh of resignation, I said, "What's going on? What did he do?"

She shook her head. "He's just being nitpicky about

everything. He's making us clock out just to use the bathroom. And if we even go a minute over our lunch break he issues a formal write up. He said something about a point system and every violation is one point. And like after three violations you're on probation and then most likely fired."

"What?" I hissed. My head was whirling. "Point system. That's crazy. What is he even talking about? And what's this about clocking out for bathroom breaks? Patrick has a bladder issue and uses the bathroom every five minutes."

"I know. I know. It's so ridiculous. I'm a nervous wreck now. That's why I'm out here smoking. And he threatened to take away our smoke breaks. And of course, we have to clock out to take one."

I shook my head. "He's worse than I thought he would be."

She nodded. "Yep." And then took a long draw on her cigarette. She quickly looked at her watch, said, "Oh crap," and tossed the half-finished cigarette on the ground and stomped it out.

"I'm already a minute over," She hurried past me and I followed her inside. As soon as we turned the corner, Mr. Baxter was there waiting. He had a smug look on his face.

"Your break ended two minutes ago," he said to Lucy.

She gulped visibly and said, "I'm so sorry. It won't happen again."

"It was my fault," I piped in. "I was talking to Lucy about some company policies and she took time out of her break to answer my questions. So, it's my fault she's late."

"Lucy's an adult. She's a big girl. She can tell the time. Late is late. No excuses. I have to write you up."

I could see that Lucy was about to tear up, and I instantly felt terrible.

"Again, I just want to mention that it was NOT her fault," I growled. "If you want to write anyone up, then it should be me since it wasn't her fault."

"I don't like your tone," Mr. Baxter said with a snarl. "And don't worry. I'm going to write you both up. How's that sound?"

Before I could say a word he turned and strolled away, heading towards his office.

Lucy looked ready to cry. "I really need this job," she said, her voice barely a whisper.

"It's just one violation, right? It'll be fine." I tried to sound reassuring, but I understood her plight. We were both single mothers just trying to live our lives.

She teared up then and said with half a sob, "I can barely afford to take care of my bills now. If he fires me, I don't know what I'll do."

I instantly reached out to her and gave her a reassuring hug briefly before letting her go, "It'll be okay. Don't cry."

I kept an arm around her shoulder as I led her back to our station in customer service. She quickly reached for a tissue and patted at her eyes while I accessed the sign-in system and signed us both in.

She sniffled a little but was no longer crying. "Thanks for being so nice."

"You don't have to thank me for being a decent human being."

"Yeah, I do, because apparently, this world is full of horrible people. My ex and our current boss to name a few."

"Gosh, don't you wish there was a way to divorce your boss?"

"There is... it's called quitting." We both laughed and then a customer appeared.

For the next four hours, I didn't see Mr. Baxter so work wasn't that bad. I was still tense the whole time because I thought at any moment that he would pop up to accuse us of doing something wrong.

Mo wasn't in which was strange. He never missed a day of work.

"Hey, Lucy, do you know where Mo is today?"

"I think his wife is sick. Or maybe she has relatives coming into town. I can't remember which, but he had to leave almost as soon as he arrived today."

"Hmmm, I hope everything's okay."

"Hello, ladies," Mr. Baxter said, suddenly appearing from the hallway that our customer service was near. "Ms... oh, I'm sorry, *Mrs.* Duran, can I see you in my office, please?"

I looked at Lucy and then back at him. "Why? I didn't do anything wrong." I was immediately on the defensive.

"That remains to be seen. My office now, Mrs. Duran."

He turned away then and I looked back at Lucy who looked at me. "What's going on?" I mouthed to her, she just shrugged and frowned deeply.

I turned around and followed him into his office. He motioned for me to sit down.

"So what is this all about?"

"Mo has been let go."

"What?"

"He was no longer needed." He cleared his throat and slid an envelope towards me. I took it and looked at him questioningly.

"I'm afraid we're going to have to let you go, as well."

"What? You can't do this."

He seemed to be enjoying himself. "I can. And I am. We're downsizing your department and no longer have room for you here. You have until the end of the day."

My head was spinning. I couldn't believe what he

was saying. "But but but I need this job. I have a daughter who relies on me—"

"Save the sob story. You should have thought of that before your insubordination the other day."

I went from feeling blindsided to feeling furious. I narrowed my eyes. "My insubordination? You mean standing up to you? Well, you know what, since I'm being fired anyway, I'll show you insubordination."

I stood up and he stood up too.

I didn't know what I planned to do. Hit him in the head with the stapler on his desk and run? Take off my shoe and throw it at him? Punch him in the face? I figured assault wouldn't look good on my next resume, so I forced myself to not hit him, but boy was I tempted.

He must have realized that because he stepped back slightly.

"Get out of my office. Forget the end of the day. I want you out of here now."

"You're nothing but a pissant, no-balls, bully." Okay, so when I said I wouldn't assault him, I meant physically assault him. Verbal assault wouldn't get me arrested.

"That's it. I'm calling security."

Okay. Maybe I was wrong. Maybe verbal assault could potentially get me arrested. But I wasn't going to back down. I spent my whole life backing down and doing what was expected of me. I hadn't even asked for anything in my divorce because I'd fostered hopes that if

I 'played nice', Tom would regret divorcing me and would come back to me. And look where that had gotten me...

"Call security. I don't care. I'm fired anyway, so I hope you don't mind if I do this," I said kicking my chair which knocked his cup of coffee off his desk and straight onto his shoe.

"Are you crazy? That was fresh coffee." He looked at me as if I'd lost my mind.

That felt good, so I started knocking other things off his desk. By the time security showed up, I was in full rampage mode and was kicking, shouting, and tearing his office apart.

"Get her out of here," he yelled as security grabbed me by my arm.

I knocked their hands off and said, "Let go of me. He's the one you should be dragging out of here."

"Come on, Dana," said one of the guards who I'd known since I started working at Primrose. "I don't want to have to call the cops," he whispered.

I sighed and let him escort me out. Lucy and Patrick looked on. Lucy looked despondent and Patrick looked highly amused.

"See you, Pat," I called as I left.

He gave me a big smile and a thumbs up. Clearly, I'd made Patrick proud. I huffily got into my car and then all my bravado disappeared as the enormity of the situation weighed on me. Great. Just great. Now I was an unemployed single mom again. I felt that no matter how hard I tried, I just kept failing Meredith in every way that mattered. Not knowing what to do, I wiped at the tears falling down my cheeks and began to drive.

5

I didn't feel like being alone. But I was grateful Meredith wasn't home to see me in such a disaster state. For once, I was actually glad that she was at her father's house.

On a whim, I decided to head over to Piper's place. She worked from home so I figured she would be around to lend a sympathetic ear.

I knocked on her door and sniffled a little, trying not to cry. As the door open, I arranged my face into a sad smile.

My face went from smiling to surprise. Instead of Piper, Carter was standing there. He had on no shoes and no shirt. He was just wearing a pair of low-slung shorts. I'd been right. He had filled out a lot since college. His body was chiseled, all wiry muscle in all the right places.

"What are you doing here?" I said as he stood back and gestured for me to come in.

"Well, I was working out..."

"You know what I mean. Where's Piper?"

"New York. She said something about meeting up with her translation partner. She's going to be gone all weekend. She asked me to housesit."

I pouted. "Why did she ask you and not me?"

He shrugged. It was a simple movement, but a sexy one... one that emphasized his beautiful shoulders. He crossed his arms across his chest, "I don't know... maybe because you have a kid and you work weekends."

I plopped down on the couch and sighed deeply. "It's Tom's weekend and I'm no longer employed. Not that Piper knows that since I was just fired like ten minutes ago."

"Fired?" he asked, sitting down next to me.

I nodded, and the tears started to flow freely then. Carter pulled me into his arms and just let me cry. I wasn't good with change and I felt overwhelmed by all the topsy-turvy ups and downs I was enduring lately. Life was being so cruel. Just when I thought I'd my footing, I would slip up and fail again. I was sick of it.

"I feel like such a failure," I mumbled into his shoulder.

"You're not a failure. Tell me what happened."

I told him everything. He listened while I kept my head pressed against his chest.

"Your boss, sorry former boss, is just a terrible person. That wasn't something you could control."

I pulled my head up and sniffled. "I know. But still, I feel like I'm failing Meredith. I want so much more for her than just this—" I gestured aimlessly. "You know?"

He shook his head. "No. I don't know what you mean. She's happy. One of the happiest kids I've ever met."

"She's resilient that's all."

"Stop underestimating your parenting skills. Yeah, some people are just naturally resilient, but you played a pretty important role in making her feel loved and secure. And you shouldn't underestimate that."

I shook my head, unconvinced.

"You don't understand."

"Really?" his reply was sharp, and I wanted to bite my tongue. Carter had also been a child of divorced parents.

"I'm sorry, I didn't mean that."

He shrugged. "It's okay. Divorce sucks, no matter how old you are, but trust me when I say Meredith is fine. She's thriving."

"Thanks for that," I said, suddenly feeling a little uncomfortable being so close to Carter. I could smell him. He smelled so nice.

He reached out and slowly touched my face. "You're too hard on yourself."

I nodded. "I know. I just feel all this pressure to get everything right. I just don't want to think that I'm ruining her life."

He shook his head again. "Not a chance. Anyone who knows you is blessed to have you in their lives. You're easy to love."

Carter was so sincere. I knew he meant every word he said. When he looked at me I saw how his eyes were full of emotion. In college, he'd always kept things friendly, but his look today was different. Underneath it was a layer of desire and tenderness I couldn't ignore.

He wanted me. But what would be our excuse this time? We didn't have a reason to 'fake' a relationship. This time there would be no excuses, no pretenses. His kiss, his touch, had stirred a desire in me that I'd ignored all too long. I'd convince myself that being desired hadn't been important in my marriage, that being held and kissed were for newlyweds and young people… as if I were sooooo old. But I'd been making excuses so that I wouldn't feel bad about feeling inadequate.

I wasn't feeling inadequate now. In fact, I didn't feel insecure at all. I felt bold. What did I have to lose? If Carter had proved anything to me almost eight years ago, it was that he could be trusted with more than just my deepest secrets, but with my body as well.

I'm not sure which one of us reached out first, but we were a tangle of limbs soon enough.

I couldn't even think clearly as his hands made their way to my breasts, freeing them from my bra as he shoved my shirt out of the way. I remembered the feel of those hands. It had been a long time. And I reacted the same way as I did back then. I arched my back as his palms were replaced by his lips.

He sucked one nipple at a time, making them hard and firm. I moaned and squirmed a little bit as I felt myself becoming wet between the legs. I was already ready for him and he had only just started.

I'd forgotten what it felt like to feel desirable. And as he pulled me into his lap, I shifted my hips so that I could rub my crotch against his own. I could feel him hardening beneath me. I wiggled a little more and he groaned. We made eye contact and then he said softly, "Stand up."

I did as I was told, and he unzipped and rid me of my jeans. He then hooked his fingers in the waistband of my panties and slowly pulled them down my legs.

I reached up as he undressed me below and took off my shirt and unhooked my bra, until I stood there nude in front of him.

"You're still so beautiful," he said reaching for me.

I let him take my hand and I expected him to tug me towards him, but he didn't. He took my hand and placed a kiss on my palm. A gentle, loving kiss that made me shudder. And then he did pull me closer, lowering me into his lap and kissing my lips, my cheeks.

When he reached my collarbone, I gasped. The light kisses he trailed there made me shudder and for the first time, I realized this wasn't just sex for Carter. No. This was making love.

My body stiffened. I could do sex, but I wasn't ready for emotions. And of course, he noticed. And pulled away.

"You okay?"

"Yeah," I said. "I just—"

"What?"

"This is a one-time event... no strings attached, okay?"

He looked away from me then and slid his hands lovingly down my hips and then settled them around my waist before bringing his eyes up to mine. It was as if he was considering something and wanted to take his time over it.

"Whatever you want, Dana," he finally said.

I leaned over and kissed him then and he played with my nipples, taking a breast in each hand. I gasped when he roughly pinched them. I liked it and found myself asking him to do it again.

He complied, but apparently, he had other things in

mind, as he pulled me out of his lap, sat me on the edge of the couch and then kneeled in front of me.

I didn't understand what he was doing, until he parted my thighs, pulled my hips forward and placed his face between my parted legs.

"Carter," I gasped as his warm mouth settled on my sex.

He slowly licked between my folds, making me scream, before he began to lick my clit. His tongue felt rough and he applied just enough pressure to make me gush in pleasure. I gripped his head and laid my back against the couch, spreading my legs wider to grant him more access.

I was really wet now, and he lapped at me, licking at my wetness. And as he played with my clit with his tongue, he brought up one hand and began to finger me. I squirmed.

"Carter, oh god, Carter—"

"Do you like that?"

I couldn't even answer as he slid another finger into me and then buried his head back between my legs.

I came, arching my back. "Carter!"

He pulled my hips forward even more and pushed my thighs apart. I came again as he kissed and licked, making me shiver and my thighs ache.

Silently, he stood up. And with heavy lids, I looked up at him as he pushed his shorts down. I felt myself growing wetter as a memory I'd forbidden myself from recalling for years surfaced.

After all these years, I would have Carter inside me again.

But the circumstances were different now. I was free to enjoy this moment and so without a smidgen of guilt, I reached out and grabbed his member. I stroked his cock and pulled him towards me. I pulled him into my mouth, greedily sucking the tip while my hand moved up and down his shaft. I took more and more of him inside my mouth and licked and sucked him, feeling him harden even more at the feel of my warm mouth around his thick, long cock.

And then abruptly, he pulled my head away.

I lay down on the couch and wantonly opened my legs as wide as I could, inviting him to take what I happily offered.

He didn't hesitate as he settled on top of me, engulfing me in the warmth of his body. I adjusted under his weight and wrapped my legs around his hips.

I could feel his cock against my opening. It was pushing against my folds, when he stopped abruptly and raised his eyes to mine.

"I don't have a condom."

"It doesn't matter," I said. "I'm on birth control." It was habitual now and I continued to take it even after my divorce.

He didn't need any more reassuring as he pulled my hips closer and gently sheathed his entire sex into mine.

"Mmmmmm," I moaned as we stayed like that, connected, but not moving and then slowly he did just that.

He moved his hips just a little, pulling himself out of my wetness. And then he pushed slowly back in, making me shake as I tightened my thighs around his hips, and dug my heels in his behind.

I went to raise my arms around his neck, but he took my hands and pinned them right above my head, holding me down as he had his way with me, shoving into my wetness.

It felt aggressive and wanton and it was exactly what I wanted and needed. I closed my eyes and just enjoyed the feel of his cock, pushing into me, stretching me.

I felt him release one of my hands and so, I began to fondle my own breasts and nipples as he thrust in and out of me.

The pleasure was building, my heart rate picked up, my inner muscles began to tighten, and then my whole body tensed as I orgasmed.

I couldn't breathe, think, or move, as my orgasm took over my entire being. I could feel my inner muscles clenching and then unclenching around Carter's sex.

But he wasn't done yet and as I lay gasping for air, he pulled out of me.

"Turn over," he commanded. I opened my eyes, not realizing that I'd closed them, and saw that he was still very erect.

He began to rub his cock, that was still wet from penetrating my sex, while he looked at my body.

"Turn over," he repeated lustfully, his voice nothing but a soft whisper.

I did as he said, slowly rolling over until I was on my knees. I looked over my shoulder behind me and watched him as he kept one hand on his cock and used the other one to open me. He slid a finger into me and my hips bucked.

I grabbed the arm of the couch and planted my hands there, just in time, as Carter slowly pushed into me, stretching me yet again and I shook at the feel of his dick entering my quivering wetness.

Just like before, he didn't bother going slow. He grabbed my hips and pulled me back, bringing my sex onto his cock over and over again, changing up the tempo and rhythm, but not pulling completely out.

I started moaning and I could hear his breathing quicken, until we were both panting each other's names with every single one of his thrusts.

He surprised me then by reaching around and playing with my clit as he penetrated me from behind. I didn't want to come again so soon, but who was I kidding? Carter was completely in control. I was just a willing bystander.

I could feel my sex seizing up around his cock, squeezing him, trying to keep him deep inside. And just like that I began to come, this time shaking.

He groaned and leaned over to place kisses down my spine, but then the gentleness was gone as he pushed into me over and over, gripping my hips as he sheathed himself in me as far as he could go. He stretched me and filled me in a way Tom never could, and I came again as Carter grunted one last time before filling me with his seed, thrusting a little as he came hard.

He pulled out immediately and I collapsed down on the couch, spent, but satisfied.

My eyes were closed, and I could feel Carter's hand rubbing my hip, lazily up and down. I don't know if I dozed off, but abruptly I opened my eyes, when I heard him give a gruff chuckle. He was sitting right next to me, staring down at me with amusement.

"What?" I said, my voice surprising me. I sounded drunk. Drunk with lust, obviously, I thought to myself.

"You have a dopey smile on your face."

"No, I don't," I said.

"Yes, you do."

"Whatever," I said, trying to wipe the stupid grin off my face.

"Don't be embarrassed. I like that I made you smile."

I felt myself blushing. "You did a lot more than make me smile."

"Don't I know it," he said, wiggling his brows and making me giggle.

I tossed a throw pillow at him that I found tucked under my butt. He easily dodged it and pulled me into his arms.

He held me in his arms and placed his head on the top of mine.

We sat like that silently, me enjoying the feeling of him holding me. But now that we were not having sex, I had to deal with the consequences of our actions. I didn't want to. I just wanted to pretend all this was no big deal, but it was a big deal. It was a huge deal. We'd yet again crossed the threshold of being just friends.

I tried not to think of that one time years ago when I'd showed up at his dorm room. I tried to forget what had happened between us that night and what it said about me. About me as a person. And what it said about my morals or lack thereof.

"What are you thinking about?" he asked me, thankfully pulling me away from my own thoughts.

"Nothing…" I lied. "What about you?"

After a long pause, he said, "I'm thinking that we're terrible people, because not only did we destroy Piper's couch, but we have our bare-naked butts on it."

I hadn't thought of that.

"Oh my gosh. Do you think she'll notice?" I said sitting up and looking around. We'd kind of made a mess of the whole living room and I hadn't even noticed. The couch wasn't where it had originally been. The rug was crooked. Throw pillows were everywhere and the cushions of the couch were askew.

And then to our horror, the front door opened.

I screamed and tried to hide behind Carter. Carter, being the gentleman that he was tried to hide me behind him, and in the hurry to get out of sight of whoever was coming in through the door, he accidentally hit me in the eye with his elbow and I accidentally kneed him in the crotch.

So that's how Piper found us—Carter grimacing with his hand on his crotch and me holding my eye, naked on her couch.

She stared at us and dropped her bags, "Oh my God, you freaks. Put on some clothes and get your nasty butts off my couch."

* * *

TEN MINUTES LATER, I made myself step out of the shower. I'd grabbed my clothes and sprinted into the bathroom after Piper's shocking arrival.

I sheepishly dried off and put on my clothes and then peeked outside where I could hear Piper laughing. I didn't hear Carter's voice. I wondered about that as I made my way out.

"You're ridiculous," she giggled as I entered the living room and I thought she was talking to me when I saw that she was actually on the phone with someone.

She realized I was there and gave me a pointed look. And then pointed at a seat at her dining room table. Uh oh. I was in trouble, I thought, as I sat down at the table.

"I gotta go. I have to take care of some business. Call you later," she said ending her conversation.

I looked around and to distract her from the conversation I knew I couldn't avoid, said, "Where's Carter?"

"Gone. He mumbled an apology and then hightailed it out of here."

"Smart guy," I joked even though part of me was irrationally upset that he could just, well, leave after what we'd just done... several times... on Piper's couch.

Speaking of which. "I'll pay to have your couch cleaned."

Piper made a face. "Are you kidding me? I'm getting rid of it. There's no way I can look at it now without thinking of your butts on it."

"I'm sorry," I squeaked. "Really, really, sorry."

She sat down heavily across from me and gave me a disapproving look. "You should be. I really liked that couch. You two could have at least played hide the sausage on my bed. That way I could just change my sheets."

I turned bright red and said, "Hide the sausage?"

She giggled and then so did I. Our fits of giggles turned into full-on laughter.

"Oh my god, you should have seen your face when I walked in," she said, gasping out the words between giggles. "You were holding your eye and he was holding his crotch. If I hadn't been so startled, I would have laughed. What the hell kind of sex were you guys having? When I have sex I never end up with a penis in my eye. I hate to say it, but I think you guys are doing it all wrong. You might need to take sex ed again."

I almost fell off the chair laughing. When I could finally breathe, I said, "We were trying to hide, but we got tangled in our rush and I ended up kneeing his nether regions and he ended up elbowing me in my eye."

Piper looked unconvinced. "Likely story."

I laughed again and then my mood grew serious. "I guess I should explain what was going on…"

"Explain what? You two had sex. That's pretty obvious."

I blushed again, "No… I mean… well, yeah, but…"

Piper looked at me confused. "Umm… it was bound to happen sometime."

"What?"

She looked at me again, this time her expression

dubious. "Carter always had a thing for you. I always thought you guys would eventually end up together. Sometimes I felt like a third wheel with you two. You guys were just always so close."

"What?" I said again, shaking my head as if to clear it. "You always thought we would end up together? But we were just friends back then," I said, and then I instantly felt bad. Piper didn't know what had happened all those years ago and I felt bad keeping her out of the loop, but I didn't want her to know the type of person I could be. I didn't want her to know that her friend was capable of infidelity.

"Come on, Dana. You had to notice. He adored you. And he was pissed when you started dating Tom. And even more pissed when you married him."

"But he came to my wedding—"

"To save face. It would have looked bad if he hadn't shown up."

"And he brought a date—"

"Of course he did. If the love of your life was your best friend and he was marrying someone else, wouldn't you want someone with you to soften the blow?"

I put up my hand. "Wait a minute. Love of his life? You're way overthinking this, Piper."

"No. I'm not exaggerating. Carter's always loved you. Do you really think it's a coincidence that he came back into town after your divorce?"

I nodded. "Well, yeah."

She looked at me as if I were the stupidest person in the world. "I can assure you that Carter would have happily spent the rest of his life saving orphans in far off places of the world, or whatever he was doing, if he hadn't heard you had gotten divorced."

"You're giving me way too much credit. Carter loves me like you love a friend. You know?"

"Really?" Piper said giving me a look. "So are you saying that what you and he did on my couch earlier was just the work of two friends?"

She had a point. I wasn't going to tell her that. It was time to avoid the subject.

"What are you doing home so early? Carter said you weren't expected back until later this weekend."

"Well," she said with a big smile on her face. "Morgan is coming back into town."

"Morgan?"

"My magician lover. Not that we've gotten down and dirty like you and Carter…"

"Piper—"

"What?"

"Can we just pretend that what you saw didn't happen?"

She sighed, "I'm the one that had to endure seeing the naked bodies of both my friends… so spare me."

I grimaced. "Sorry."

She said as if she were a schoolmarm, "You should be."

My phone began ringing and I jumped up to find it. My purse was somehow wedged under the coffee table. I gave it one hard yank and flew into the couch as I unearthed it.

I dug through my purse searching for my phone, knowing that the ringing would stop in a few seconds and worried that it was Meredith. When I finally found it at the bottom of my purse, the caller had already hung up. It was a missed call from Carter.

I wasn't ready to talk to him yet. I just couldn't.

"Who was it?" Piper asked.

"Carter," I said softly.

"So are you guys an item now and I'm just the last to know? First you make out at my party and now this," she said, gesturing to her couch which was still a little disheveled. "And don't try to tell me you guys were just pretending... that might have been a likely excuse before, but definitely not now."

I blushed. "We're not an item. We're just friends... we've always been friends..."

"Friends that just happen to have sex with each other?"

"It was a one-time lapse in judgment," I lied. "Carter and I are just friends. I'm not ready to be in a relationship with anyone. I mean, your brother really left me feeling like a… a… nobody."

Her face instantly changed. Gone was the teasing smile. In her eyes was sympathy. "I'm sorry. My brother's a dick. I wish you'd never had dated him, let alone married him."

"It wasn't all bad", I said pitifully. "I got Meredith."

"And Meredith is an amazing little girl, but there's nothing wrong with wanting more for yourself. You deserve to move on, too, Dana."

"I know that. I just… can't…"

"Well, it seems like you're off to a good start," she said teasing again.

I sighed. "What happened between me and Carter was just a spur of the moment thing. A mistake. I was feeling emotional. He was really comforting. One thing led to another—"

"And you guys found yourself butt naked on my couch. Yeah, I get naked on my couch with Carter all the time when I feel emotional," she mocked. I narrowed my eyes at her and she sighed. "Fine. If you want to pretend nothing is going on between you and him… but hey, as his friend, could you not call it a mistake around him?"

I gulped. "But it was—"

Her face tightened, and she had a look on her face that I wasn't familiar with. Was she angry with me?

"Are you angry with me?"

She shrugged. "I'm trying not to be. But Carter loves you, Dana."

"He's my friend—"

"He's OUR friend, but you broke his heart when you chose Tom over him."

I felt my world fall out of focus. "So, you know what happened all those years ago?"

She nodded.

I wanted to hide my face.

"I'm sorry,"

"Why are you apologizing?"

"I cheated on your brother with our best friend."

She shrugged. "You call it a mistake, I call it karma."

"What?"

"Tom was a serial cheater."

Now I was in shock. My head started to hurt, and I felt like I could barely breathe. "What? Tom cheated on me? And you knew? And you never told me?"

I didn't know what upset me more: knowing that Tom had been unfaithful to me or knowing that Piper had known the whole time and never told me.

Piper looked away. "I'm sorry—"

I wasn't ready to hear this and I was determined not to stick around to hear any more. I rose from my seat at the table and silently gathered my things.

"Dana, wait, come on, I didn't know what to do, I knew you wouldn't believe me if I told you. You thought the sun rose and set on Tom. You wouldn't have believed me."

I knew she was right. Up until he'd divorced me I'd put Tom on a pedestal. He could do no wrong in my eyes. I'd always chosen to believe the best of him even when he always just showed me his worst. But I still felt betrayed by Piper. It seemed like we were all keeping secrets. Piper knew about Tom's infidelity and had never told me. Carter apparently always harbored feelings for me and I'd never told Piper that we'd slept together in college. Some friends we were.

"I can't talk about this now," I said as she grabbed my shoulder to stop me from leaving.

"Don't be angry with me. I was just a kid. I didn't know what to do."

"Tell me something. Was he cheating on me while I was married to him? I mean once a cheater always a cheater, right?"

She shrugged. "I honestly don't know. And I swear I would have told you—"

"Really? You really expect me to believe that. I thought you were better than this, Piper," I said, my voice dripping with animosity. I knew I was lashing out. I was angry and upset and I felt betrayed by everyone who was important in my life. The only people I'd thought I could trust apparently kept secrets from me deliberately. I knew I had no right to fault them, but I had to direct my pain and anger towards something, and that something was actually someone. I couldn't yell at Tom or Carter, so I yelled at Piper.

"Like I said, I'm sorry. If I could do it all over again, I would have told you, Dana. But you were so in love with him. You wouldn't have listened to me." Her voice sounded raw and I could tell she was getting choked up. "Please tell me you understand why I didn't say anything. I just didn't want to jeopardize our friendship by you thinking I was a liar."

"Too late," I said with no emotion in my voice.

Piper looked as if I slapped her. Hesitantly she said, "Well, I'm here for you, if you want to talk…"

I didn't say a word in reply; I just shrugged and walked away, feeling that in more ways than one, I'd lost both of my best friends in one day.

"Mom, come on, wake up. I'm going to be late to school."

I groaned as I made myself sit up. I pushed my hair out of my face and sighed before falling back into the pillows.

"Mom, please… you're going to make me late and then I'll be embarrassed and sad and end up in juvenile detention because of neglect."

I sat up instantly. Where had she gotten those crazy ideas from? "Have you been watching TV for adults again?"

She shook her head innocently. "Nope. Danny Schultz told me his cousin is in juvie for talking back to his parents and peeing on the neighbor's front yard."

I frowned. "Honey, can you talk to someone else at school besides Danny Schultz?"

She shrugged. "Sure. But I talk to everyone. It's just that Danny is never boring."

"You got that right," I mumbled to myself.

"His mom is a parole officer. She gives sandwiches to criminals and sometimes she lets the really nice ones sleep on her couch."

Now I was definitely awake. "No sleepovers at Danny's place."

She giggled. "Oh Mom, you're so silly. Dad would NEVER let me go on a sleepover at a boy's house. No way, no how."

The way she said it was adorable but at the mention of her father I instantly became furious. After Piper's confession, I went from thinking of Tom as the one who got away to the one who could have possibly given me an STD or STI, whatever the kids called sexually transmitted diseases nowadays.

I figured I'd been lucky all those years that my gyno recommended I get tested for everything even though I'd reassured her that I could completely trust my husband.

Joke's on me, I could trust him as far as I could throw him. That asshole.

"Let's get you dressed," I said, climbing out of bed and pushing thoughts of Tom way out of my head.

Meredith looked at me as if I'd lost my mind. "I'm dressed, Mom."

I finally took a good look at her and realized that she was right. My phone rang and I looked to see who was calling. It was Piper.

It had been a few days since the incident at her house and I was steadily avoiding her calls as well as Carter's.

I was irrationally furious with Piper. And when it came to Carter, I didn't know how I felt, so I was avoiding his phone calls too.

"Alright kiddo, apparently you're more of an adult than I am. Teach me your ways," I said, bowing to her.

She laughed. "You're too funny, Mommy. But now's not the time for jokes. We have things to do. Get dressed. Fast!"

She gave me a sweet smile and headed out. I stood there with my mouth agape and then laughed. Who was this bossy elementary schooler and what had she done with my sweet daughter?

Bemused, I did as I was told and then together we headed to the car.

I was asking her about her class project when she cut me off saying, "Why aren't you answering Auntie Piper's calls? She's called you like six times and you haven't picked up. Aren't you guys friends anymore? Best of friends?"

I looked at her through my rearview mirror and instantly felt terrible. Her voice held so much concern. My heart went out to my considerate, thoughtful, sensitive daughter who was a way better person than I ever would be. Instead of her learning from me, it would serve me well to learn from her. Her viewpoint of the world wasn't necessarily innocent, but she was a practical person who didn't hold grudges or harbor any ill-will towards others. While I'd spent the past year bitter and angry, she had gracefully accepted that her life as she knew it was changing, but instead of being angry and uncompromising, she had tried to make the best of out a less than desirable situation.

At that moment, I knew I had to do better. So far the only thing I managed to accomplish was to alienate one of my best friends, ignore the other, and get fired.

What type of example was I setting for Meredith? I was a mess. My life was a mess and it was all because of my choices. I vowed from that moment on to make better choices. Beginning now…

"You know, you're amazing," I said to her, totally off topic, but I wanted her to know how special she was to me.

She grinned. "So are you, but you're trying to change the subject."

"Gosh, you're a smarty-pants."

"Just like my mother," she said in a sing-song voice.

I guffawed. How could I be in a bad mood when I had such a great kid?

"Well, Auntie Piper and I had an argument."

"About what?"

Yikes. I didn't know how to answer that one. What should I say? Well, your father cheated on me for years and I knew nothing about it. But it's cool, we're even since I cheated on your father with the guy who is now your principal.

Nope. I wasn't going to say that. That was even too much daytime talk show-like drama for me to take.

"Sometimes adults have disagreements."

"Oh," she said sadly. "You guys had a fight?"

Her voice was so sad. I instantly rushed to reassure her. "No… just a little fight. About something that happened a long, long, long time ago."

"If it happened a long time ago, then why are you still mad now?"

I sighed to myself. Again, Meredith was wiser and a better person than her mother. Why was I angry with Piper?

I could lie to myself and say I was unhappy with her because she had lied to me by omission, but nope, that's not why I was angry.

It was what she said about me not believing her. She had been right. I'd convinced myself that every piece of evidence of Tom's infidelities had all been in my mind. The text messages he received when we were together. The excuses for why I could never visit him at his apart- ment. There had been so many red flags and I'd ignored them all. Well, all but one. And the one I hadn't ignored had directly led me to finding solace in Carter's arms.

But now I wondered if Tom's infidelities had just been my excuse to run to Carter. I didn't want to think too deeply about that and instead focused on Meredith's questions.

"Sometimes adults do really stupid things. And you made me realize that being mad at your Auntie Piper is really stupid."

She nodded like a sage satisfied by a deduction her student had made.

"Exactly, Mom. So just tell Auntie Piper you're sorry for being mad and then everything will be okay again."

"You think so?" I said, needing reassurance and laughing at myself from getting it from a five-year-old.

"Mom, it's Auntie Piper. She's like the nicest person in the world," Meredith said, rolling her eyes as if I were the stupidest person in the world.

"You're right."

"And I don't think she's mad at you anymore because if she was mad at you she wouldn't call you ALL the time."

I laughed. "You're so smart. You know that?"

"Yep. You tell me that every day."

We pulled up to the drop-off line and I was careful not to hit anybody this time. I waved goodbye to her as she climbed out the car.

"Have a great day, sweetheart!"

"You too, Mom. Have fun at work."

I tried not to grimace at her parting words. I hadn't told her that I'd been fired. I knew she would worry about me and I couldn't have that.

I was scared that Carter would be waiting for me and planned to ambush me and force me to talk to him in the drop-off line, but he was nowhere to be found.

I breathed a sigh of relief and drove off. I could only deal with fixing up one relationship at a time. I would start off with Piper first and then contact Carter, I told myself.

It felt good to have a plan, but my first order of business needed to be finding a job.

I'd already submitted at least fifty job applications over the past few days and I hadn't received one call back. But I knew that was the norm. I just needed to work harder or network. Whatever it was people did to find a job. I felt so foolish. I didn't even know how to find a job because my husband had just taken care of me. And once he stopped taking care of me, I had to find out how to do all of this on my own. It made me feel so ridiculous.

But enough about my own insecurities, I needed to just suck it up and ask for help. I found a number to a temp agency that was hiring and immediately submitted an application online. To my surprise, I got a call an hour later.

"Hi, Can I speak to Dana Duran?"

"Yes, this is Dana," I said nervously jumping off the couch where I'd been binging on Netflix while continuing to fill out various applications.

I paced the floor, hoping that I sounded professional. I also happened to have a mouth full of dark chocolate almonds in my mouth. Dark chocolate was the only treat I allowed myself to have often. I told myself it was okay because dark chocolate was rumored to be healthy and well, almonds were healthy too… just covered in yumminess.

"We have an administrative assistant position available in the downtown area. We're trying to fill the position immediately. If you would be interested in interviewing for it, we have a spot available for you at four pm today."

Four? I had to pick up Meredith at four.

"Is four the only time available?"

"Hold for me. I'll check."

I started pacing the floor again while I waited on the line. The hold music was 80's pop. I started singing along to "Oh Mickey," when the secretary came back on the line.

"I'm sorry, four o'clock is the only time Michelle has available."

I had to think quickly. I chewed on my lip. Our savings were already running dry. I needed a new job and I needed one stat or I would have to start selling my body on the street corner for oatmeal and chocolate covered almonds.

"I'll be there. Can I get the address?"

Five minutes later, I was off the phone, but I had no idea what I was going to do about Meredith's pick-up time.

I didn't want to call Tom. And there was no way I was going to explain to Becca that I was going to a job interview. I knew she would immediately feel sorry for me and ask me if I was poor.

Instead, I reached for the phone and called the one person I knew would have no problem with my last-minute request.

Hours later, I pulled up to a small craftsman style home that stood out from the rest of the neighborhood just because of its size. It seemed that the neighborhood was being regentrified. Giant townhomes that clearly didn't belong on such small plots of land dotted the neighborhood on either side. And across from the giant three-story townhomes were McMansions.

Carter's place was clearly one of the original homes

and if the outside was any indication, it seemed as if it had been recently remolded and renovated.

I opened the quaint gate that was covered in lovely ivy vines and noted the smell of midnight blooming jasmines in the air. I wondered briefly if Carter had planted them himself. There were rows of flowers on one side of his home and it was clear that they were lovingly maintained. I didn't know Carter was into gardening, I thought, but there was probably a lot I didn't know about the man that I'd considered my best friend. And who on two occasions already had been my lover.

I pushed those thoughts away as I rang his doorbell. It was dark, and the porch light shot on immediately.

"Who is it?" I heard him call through the door before he looked out the peephole.

I gave him a wane smile and said, "It's me, Dana."

I heard the doors unlocking and then finally he opened it.

"Sorry," he said with a shrug. "Can never be too careful."

"Yeah, an alien could have invaded my body and who knows what would have happened if you opened the door."

He laughed. "Still into sci-fi, I see?"

"You would be right." I looked around his home, seeking out Meredith.

"She passed out on the floor over there after I won a few games of Candyland."

I walked over to her. It looked like Carter had put a throw over her and placed one of the pillows from the couch under her head.

"She looks so peaceful," I said with a smile. I always smiled when I saw her sleeping. She always looked so innocent.

"I tried to make sure she was comfortable. I would have picked her up and moved her into the guest bedroom, but I didn't want her to wake up in a strange room and panic."

I nodded. "That was thoughtful of you."

He shrugged like it was no big deal. But it was.

"Once again, you've come to my rescue."

"That's what friends are for, right?"

I leaned against one of the columns in his home and took a moment to look around. He had a large fireplace that took up most of the living room. Some people might have considered the original brick old-fashioned, but I thought it looked homey and cozy. There was a fire burning and I sat down next to it and stretched out my feet.

Carter joined me, and we sat there for a moment not saying anything.

I started first.

"I guess we should talk about what happened the other day."

He looked towards the room where Meredith was, as if to make sure she was asleep.

"Don't worry," I said with a wry smile, "When she's asleep, she's out. She won't overhear us."

He nodded and then said, "I'm sorry for leaving abruptly."

I held my hands out in front of the fire, enjoying the warmth whilst trying to come up with something to say that felt right. But I couldn't come up with anything.

"When you sprinted to the bathroom, I just tried to get out of there as fast as I could. I felt terrible—"

"Me too," I said quickly. "I mean, we should have never have let that happen."

He looked at me quizzically. "To be clear, I feel terrible that we defiled Piper's couch. I don't have any regrets about what happened between us… do you?"

I couldn't even look at him. I didn't want to hurt him, but what other choice did I have? I guess my silence stretched too long because he began speaking again.

"I'm going to take your silence to mean you don't feel the same way."

"I didn't say that."

"You didn't say anything." He sighed. "How long are we going to do this same old dance, Dana?"

"What do you mean?" I asked, not understanding him.

"You know how I feel about you."

I turned to look at him then and he took that moment to take my hand in his. I stared into his eyes, clearly seeing love there. He looked at me in a way that Tom never did.

"I… it's not that easy for me, Carter," I said nervously, licking my lips. His eyes followed the movement.

He didn't say anything. He just reached for my face and cupped my chin in his hand. He gently stroked my face.

"I have no interest in complicating your life… I just want to be a part of it."

"You are a part of it."

"I don't want to just be your old buddy from college. Our relationship was never that simple."

"Yes, it was," I said combatively. "Until I ruined things."

"Ruined things? Being with you that night didn't ruin anything for me. Sorry if you feel differently." His words weren't angry, just matter of fact.

"I don't know how I feel. I just know what we did… back then… was wrong."

He didn't look convinced. "Is it wrong to be with the person you love?"

My heart skipped a beat and I could no longer meet

his eyes. I knew. I always knew. But our timing had always been off. I would never forget when I met Carter. I'd instantly said to myself that he was the type of guy that I wanted to marry.

But he hadn't seemed interested in me and he had had plenty of girls vying for his attention. I'd settled with just being his friend. And he had been a great friend and I'd made myself not want anything with him more than friendship. And then I'd met Tom and figured my infatuation with Carter would just disappear if I dated Tom more, until eventually Tom and I were an item.

I'd just stuck with the script I thought my life had written me. Up until that night... that night that I'd found a pair of panties that weren't mine in Tom's car.

I could remember that night as if it were yesterday. I'd borrowed Tom's car to pick up something to eat. I'd dropped my wallet on the passenger seat and of course, since I was a reckless driver back then, I'd taken a corner too fast and my wallet had disappeared under the seat.

While looking for it, my hand had closed over something that felt like paper, but it was cold. Upon further investigation, I found out that it was an empty condom wrapper and lying right next to it had been a pair of panties.

And they were definitely not mine.

I'd been so upset that I'd driven like a mad woman out of the drive-thru line and headed straight to the campus.

I'd marched up the stairs of my dorm, threw open my door, and proceeded to scream at the top of my lungs at Tom who had been sleeping in my bed. He had sat up, totally unaware of what was going on.

But I had the evidence. I pulled the panties and condom wrapper out of my pocket and tossed them at him.

He easily dodged them and then picked them up.

"You're a fucking cheater! How could you do this to me?" I'd yelled, slamming the door behind me. I'd heard murmurs in the hall, but I wasn't done yet. If I was going to get kicked out of the dorm for going crazy on my boyfriend, so be it.

He hadn't responded immediately. Instead, he had had the audacity to yawn and stretch, taking his time to answer me.

I'd been livid. Livid.

"Answer me," I shouted, slamming my hand down on my dresser so hard that pain radiated up my arm.

"Calm down," he said with a sigh as if I was some disobedient child that he just happened to tolerate. "I let Jeff borrow my car and apparently he had a wild night. That's not a crime."

"You're a liar," I said hotly, crossing my arms.

"Stop the name calling," he said, "I told you what happened, so you can either accept the truth or continue acting like a petulant child. Your choice."

And then like that he had tossed the two items on the floor and laid back down in my bed, facing away from me.

"That's it… that's all you have to say?" I said, my voice cracking.

"You're being emotional and childish right now," he said, finally flipping over and arrogantly placing his arms behind his head.

"Emotional and childish?" I sobbed, my anger disappearing and easily replaced by hurt. "Look what I found in your car!" I yelled, pointing at where he'd discarded the items.

"I'm done discussing this," he said, yet again flipping over. "Wake me up when you grow up."

At that moment a knock sounded on my room door. I snatched the door open and my resident advisor stood there looking concerned. There was a crowd of onlookers around, openly gawking, not even bothering to look discreet.

"Are you okay?" The resident advisor asked me. Her name was Susan and she was a sweetheart.

I looked behind me toward Tom who hadn't even bothered to face us and tried to keep additional tears from falling as I turned back to Susan.

"I'm fine. I just… I just need some air."

I stepped across the threshold and slammed my door shut, startling Susan and everyone else who looked on.

But I didn't care as I headed to the other side of campus. I cried the whole time as I walked. I'd had my suspicions. I just never had any concrete evidence. It felt like such a slap in the face. I wiped at my tears and stopped in the middle of the green to compose myself when someone called out to me.

It was Carter.

"Hey, you," he said, walking towards with me with a friend of his that I didn't know well. I instantly felt self-conscious.

I must have looked a mess because his face darkened in concern.

"What's wrong, Dana? Tell me what happened. Who do I need to kill?" he said, waving for his friend to go on without him.

"I can't—Tom—oh God." And then I slumped forward and began to sob on Carter's chest as he held me.

"Come on," he said to me. "I can't have you crying in the middle of the night on the green. What type of monster would that make me?"

"Not a monster at all in comparison to Tom."

He silently took my hand and didn't say a word about my last comment. He had never badmouthed

Tom, but he'd never praised him either. Their hate for each other was almost tangible.

I understood Carter now because suddenly I hated Tom with a passion too.

We went back to Carter's dorm room and he'd given me a cup of hot chocolate that he found in the kitchenette. He also handed me a washcloth and helped me clean my face, while I warmed my hands on the cup of chocolate.

I'd smiled up at him with a wobbly grin, trying to keep it together, telling myself not to cry.

"You don't have to put on a brave front for me," he'd said. "If you want to cry, then feel free to cry."

I took in a shaky breath. "I don't think Tom is right for me," was all I could say. It humiliated me to admit that he was cheating on me. It just meant that all this time I truly hadn't been good enough for him.

To my surprise, Carter said, "I'm glad you finally came to your senses. Because he's not right for you. He never was, and he never will be."

"I think he's cheating on me," I said, feeling safe suddenly with sharing my secret.

Carter growled, "If he's too stupid to be faithful to you, what's the point of even being with him?

I looked down at my hands and sighed. "Maybe there's more to the story. Maybe I should go back and talk to him... actually listen to his side."

I stood up and Carter reached out his hand to stop me. "Wait… he doesn't deserve you, Dana. He doesn't. Even if he isn't a cheat, he's all wrong for you."

"You always hated him."

"I don't hate him… I hate that he has you."

I was stunned. I didn't know Carter felt that way.

"If Tom isn't right for me, Carter, then who is?"

"Me," he said, standing up now and tugging me gently toward him.

"Carter, I—"

He kissed me then, stopping me from saying anything at all, and it was as if that kiss was what my body—no my entire being—was waiting for. I kissed him back, not caring about the consequences.

It felt right. Everything about touching Carter felt right.

When he had finally broken the kiss, I just stood there not knowing what to say or what to do.

"I love you, Dana. Give me a chance to make you happy," he said, tucking a hair behind my ear.

"Carter," I said hesitantly, feeling so many emotions and not able to deal with even one. I was overwhelmed. "We're friends. I don't want to ruin that."

"I love you too much to let that happen," he said before kissing me again. This time he ran his hands down my arms and pulled me up against him so that his crotch was pressing against my thigh.

Against my better judgment, I moved against it. I wanted him. I wanted him more than I'd ever wanted a man.

Slowly, we undressed each other, and I'd welcomed Carter inside me that night again and again.

My mind snapped back to the present and I realized Carter was staring at me. I think he was also recalling that night and he slowly stroked my hand. The soft, innocent touch, sent goosebumps up my hands.

"I can't talk about this now," I said softly, avoiding his last question about love.

"When are you going to stop running from me, Dana?"

I took my hand away. "I'm not running, I just want to be sure. I'm tired of making the same mistakes, of choosing wrong, I need to make better decisions, not just for me, but for Meredith too."

He was silent for a long time and he just studied me. His eyes were hard to read. I couldn't tell what he was thinking now. He was closed off.

"I respect that," he finally said. "Here, let me carry Meredith to your car for you."

I hadn't expected that change of subject. A lot had been left unsaid, but I was glad for a minor reprieve.

He effortlessly carried Meredith to my car and buckled her in. She slept through the entire process like I knew she would.

I stood outside of my car and Carter stood in front of me.

"Thanks for helping me out tonight."

"No problem. I'll do anything for you. Did you get the job?" he asked. I knew he was attempting to keep things light and I appreciated that.

I nodded. I'd aced the interview. I'd completely knocked it out the park. "It's just temporary," I said. "With the possibility of going full-time eventually."

"That's great," he said genuinely looking happy for me. "What will you be doing?"

"I'm going to be an administrative assistant for a local government office."

"Cool," he said looking surprised. "Maybe they'll let you put that marketing degree to some use."

I smiled because he remembered my major. What didn't he remember about me?

"It turns out that they need someone to work on their social media presence, so that's going to be part of my new job, so I'll get to learn a little bit about maybe digital marketing... I don't know, at least I'll learn how to use Twitter."

"I don't even have a Twitter account."

"Nor do I," I confessed and we both laughed.

Meredith stirred, and I looked at Carter apologetically.

"Let's continue this conversation later, okay? I

should get her home so she can eat and binge watch Netflix with me."

"Good parenting right there."

"I'm the best," I said facetiously, and he laughed.

He then leaned forward and placed a chaste kiss on my forehead.

"Be safe."

He walked back in then, not even waiting for my response and I climbed into the car wondering if I'd done the right thing all those years back. I couldn't undo the past, but God did I have regrets.

I drove home, deep in my own thoughts when I heard a little voice say, "He likes you, you know."

"Hey, you, what are you doing awake?" I said, caught off guard and not ready to have THAT conversation with her.

"Principal K really likes you or he wouldn't have kissed you."

I blushed. "You saw that?"

"Yep. And he always asks about you. He asks every day how you're doing."

"Well, he's my friend…"

"He wants to be your boyfriend," she said with a deep sigh. "And I think you should let him. If my mom dates the principal then I can do whatever I want."

I laughed. "Hush up, you little stinker."

She shrugged playfully. "I'm just saying…"

We pulled up into the driveway shortly after and my phone beeped as I parked. I reached for it and checked my text messages.

"How about dinner next week?" was the short and simple text from Carter.

I didn't even get a chance to think about it as Meredith said from near my shoulder. "Say yes! Say yes!"

I hadn't even heard her unbuckle herself.

I turned to argue with her when she snatched the phone from me, typed something and then jumped out the car and ran.

"Get back here, you little troublemaker! What did you send?" I yelled reaching for my phone which she had flung in the back seat.

I snatched it up and saw that she had typed yes.

I narrowed my eyes and she looked at me innocently from the front door as I gathered her bags and made my way to our porch.

"I should ground you for like a million years."

"But you won't," she said. "I'm just helping you. Trust me," she said sounding older than her age. "You'll thank me later."

I ruffled her hair and sighed, what had Meredith gotten me into?

"You know, we could have gone bowling or something."

"Nope," Carter said as he held the car door open for me. "This is our first date and I'm determined to make it as romantic and impressive as possible."

What wasn't said was that I was already impressed. He had texted me back that same night and between Meredith's ribbings, I'd found myself agreeing to dinner and a movie with Carter.

I'd been nervous all week. I hadn't known what to wear or how to dress. I didn't know if I should wear makeup and perfume.

I'd decided on both at the last minute and I think Carter approved. Who was I kidding? I knew he approved. He couldn't stop looking at how long my legs were in my mini-dress.

I'd gotten it shortly after my divorce. It had been an impulse buy once I'd heard from my very innocent daughter that she now had two mommies. If I hadn't needed to be a functional adult that weekend Meredith had told me her dad had remarried, I would have certainly gotten drunk and woken up in my own vomit in an alley. But because I was a mom, I'd just bought some expensive clothes that I could no longer afford.

I'd returned almost all of them when I'd returned to my senses, but I'd kept this one as a token of perseverance. That's what it had meant to me. And now I was actually wearing it on a date. A date with my best friend.

Who would have thought the day would come when that would happen?

"Well, I'm impressed so far." I shyly cast a glance in his direction. "You look amazing."

He laughed.

I bit my lip. "Sorry, if that doesn't sound like a very masculine compliment. I could say that you look handsome, but that sounds ways too tame."

"Amazing sounds good to me. A woman has never described me as amazing before." He then winked dramatically at me. "At least not outside of bed."

I couldn't help myself. I laughed so hard my sides began to hurt. "You're ridiculous."

He smiled. "Of course, I am. And if that's what it

takes to get you to go on date number two with me, then ridiculous it is."

"Date number two, huh? What makes you think you'll get a second date?"

"I don't know, I just have a feeling."

I smiled to myself as I leaned back against the headrest. Ensconced in the darkness of the car, I let myself relax. It was sort of nice being courted, going on a date, having someone genuinely interested in me, and I was lucky that it was someone that was also a friend. Maybe this would work out after all.

We chatted about his experiences abroad and my new job. I told him how nice the people were and how being fired had actually been a good thing, it seemed.

"Yeah, sometimes you have to be forced to make a change, you know? Like your life has to be disrupted first before you wake up and realize you can do better."

I considered his words and thought of where I would be if Tom hadn't divorced me. I would still be sitting at home, hungry for love, overweight, and unhappy. I could admit that now. I'd been unhappy. And maybe so had Tom.

But I wasn't going to focus on my divorce tonight. I wasn't going to dwell in the past, especially when my future looked so promising.

I looked over at Carter then. He paused at a stop light and looked back at me.

"What?" he said with a small smile.

I shrugged. "Oh, nothing. I'm just thinking about how much things have changed."

"Sometimes change is good," he said as he pulled off.

I nodded. "But I'm a Capricorn, so I'm not a big fan of change and I have the bad habit of self-sabotaging."

Oh, I'd just admitted more to him in the last few seconds than I'd admitted to myself in the last ten years.

"I think most people, more or less, are afraid to embrace change," he said kindly. "If you think about it, the familiar is safe. Change is scary. Sometimes it's important to be a little scared though, not everything in life should be easy."

"Ha! I wholeheartedly disagree," I said as we pulled up to a funky looking restaurant. I could hear music already and it sounded like reggae.

He stopped the car and said, "I hope you like Jamaican food."

"Never tried it."

"You're going to love it."

He quickly got out the car and made his way around to open the door for me. As I stepped out, I felt a little out of my element.

Almost everyone else was dressed casually, while I looked like I was dressed to go to a club.

I tugged at my hemline self-consciously.

Carter noticed and hooked an arm around my waist. "Stop. You look great."

"Everyone else is dressed so casually."

"They're probably going to the outdoor or bar section."

He led me inside and I could see that the building was deceptively large. We walked past an area with a bar and a live band and headed up a flight of stairs.

It was then that I saw other people dressed a lot like me. The top floor had a hostess who greeted us warmly.

She had caramel colored skin and dreadlocks that extended down her back.

"I see you have a date tonight, Carter. Who's the lucky girl?" Her accented English held a slightly British hint.

He smiled down at me as we followed behind her. "This is Dana."

Her eyebrows shot up. "The Dana? Dana from college?"

"One and only."

I didn't know what to say as we settled down at our table and she handed us a menu, giving us a big smile. "Enjoy yourselves."

"So the hostess at this restaurant knows me by name?"

He tried to look nonchalant but I knew him too well.

"Come on, spill it."

"She's the bartender on Friday nights and I might have mentioned you a time or two."

"Oh really?"

"I mean, briefly, in passing. I don't sit at the bar every night and sob into my beer pining after you."

I tried to hold back a smile. "So, is crying into your beer and sobbing over me just your Saturday activity?"

"Yeah, weekends and holidays. And maybe every other Monday," he joked.

I couldn't wipe the smile off my face as I looked at him. It felt good to be around him. It felt good to be wanted. More than that, it felt good to be loved. But that's how he felt about me. How did I feel about him?

I'd always loved Carter as a friend. And I'd thought my crush on him had faded after I began to date Tom, but maybe it hadn't faded. Maybe I'd just buried it and what happened between us back in college had been a result of all those emotions bubbling up and spilling over the surface. I'd thought that Carter had been making love to me while I'd only been having sex with him, but maybe for both of us, that act had been an act of love.

It was too much to consider thinking that I, or rather, *we'd* wasted so much time, time that we could have had together. But we had the present. And he was sitting across from me now, so it was time to do something different.

Maybe the divorce had been the push I'd needed to find myself. And maybe I would find myself much in love with Carter. I didn't believe in happily ever after. With Tom, I'd thought just 'content ever after' was good enough, but with Carter, I felt anything was possible… even a fairy tale where things worked out in my favor. Maybe tonight I would stop feeling broken, useless, and sad.

My morose thoughts didn't last long as Carter reached for my hand and said, "What do you think of the restaurant?"

It had a Caribbean vibe to it, but it was subtle. The lighting was low and soft sounds of reggae filtered through the air.

"It feels sort of magical, like one of those high-class restaurants at those Caribbean resorts."

I'd only been to one and that had been during spring break my senior year in college. I wondered if Carter remembered it as fondly as I did.

"Do you remember our senior class trip during spring break?"

He nodded. "Now that was a good time. It was my first taste of the Caribbean and it was how I became addicted to reggae."

"Addicted to reggae?"

He nodded. "I even joined a band."

"You did not."

"I did," he said with a sigh and then shook his head. "Now, to be honest, we weren't very good."

I muffled a laugh. "Who else was in the band?"

"Well there was me… and well, just me."

I couldn't hold back any longer. "A one-man band?" My sides hurt as I tried to contain my laughter.

"I had high aspirations for myself."

"More like delusions."

He reached for his phone and started looking for something. I thought my teasing had offended him and I rushed to apologize when he handed me his phone.

It was a web link and on it was a picture of a reggae album for sale. "What is this?"

"I made an album." The cover of the album was so cheesy. There were palm trees, a beach, and a silhouette of a man looking towards the setting sun. Holding back a grin was becoming impossible.

I looked at the number of stars. "Hey! You have four stars! That's impressive."

He laughed, "Not really. As soon as I released it, I had my mom, dad, stepdad, and stepmom review it under different accounts."

I chuckled. "Hey, maybe they're honest reviews."

Carter patted my hand. "You're sweet. I know it sucked but I was young and dumb."

"Well, at least you wasted your youth creating bad

music. The only thing I have to show for myself is a failed marriage."

"You're too hard on yourself."

"No. I think it's the opposite. I haven't been hard enough." I sat back and took a sip of my water that had appeared without me noticing. "I feel like I've been asleep at the wheel for years, just crashing and burning, never opening my eyes to actually figure out what I was doing or where I was going. Being here with you tonight, I don't know. Makes me feel like I used to feel, like I was able to do anything, be anybody... more than just a failed housewife."

"Hey, don't—"

"No, seriously, I was a terrible housewife. I could barely keep anything clean and my cooking skills are scary. Raising Meredith was the only thing I could get right... at least, I hope I haven't scarred her for life."

"Stop beating yourself up. Meredith is amazing and come on, a marriage takes two to makes things work. And I sincerely doubt Tom is sitting around berating himself for the role he played."

He had a point. Tom never admitted when he was wrong. I wasn't the only one that made my marriage suck. Tom had been absent, emotionless, and distant. At the end of the day, I think we both knew we shouldn't have gone down the road of matrimony, but we'd both done what was expected of us, and look how that had turned out.

"So no more negative talk," Carter said. "You need to be more positive."

"I'm like the Grouch from Sesame Street, I don't know how to be happy."

"You're not the Grouch, you're more like Elmo… or Big Bird."

"Thanks, Carter. I appreciate that. Such a sweet compliment to be compared to a giant yellow bird."

"Well, you are sort of on the tall side," he said, and I swatted him with my menu. He caught my hand and held it. We stayed like that with our hands linked until dinner arrived.

The restaurant had a seasonal menu which meant it was limited. We ordered whatever our hostess recommended which for us was almost everything.

"Oh my God, that was so, so good," I said, patting my stomach an hour later as I sat back against my chair. I was stuffed and I didn't even feel guilty about it. We'd had a mix of meat, rice, and veggie dishes. The ingredients were familiar but the spices and seasonings used transported me back to our Caribbean trip. Everything had tasted authentic and fresh and left me wanting more although I was stuffed.

"Any dessert?" Ann, our hostess asked us, as she

brought us the bill. "Our baker is Cuban, and she makes the best flan in town."

"I don't doubt it, but I'm stuffed."

She turned to Carter. "I'll take one, but to go," he said.

My eyes widened. "You still have room for dessert after all that food?" It was no exaggeration that every plate on our table was empty. We'd even eaten the vegetables that were supposed to serve as decorations on the plate.

He shrugged and gave me a smile. "I'm greedy and I have a sweet tooth."

"Aww… I'd forgotten about the sweet tooth."

We stood up and Ann mentioned something about dropping dessert off for Carter downstairs. I didn't think anything of it and then he said. "I hope you're ready for some dancing."

I really didn't think I was. My belly was too full, but dancing was my guilty pleasure while I'd been married to Tom. To relax or to feel happy, I would dance around our living room in my underwear. But dancing had always been my escape from a tense household. Growing up, I'd participated in all the free dancing gigs that I could.

In college, I'd been part of an informal dancing team and had even flirted with being a dancing major, but my mom had quickly squashed that idea.

"We didn't send you to college so that you could major in dance and be poor," my mom had said succinctly.

And so, I'd just majored in marketing, but dancing had been my passion. Ironically, I hadn't pursued my passion and I'd still ended up poor.

The music was louder now, and the band was playing classic Bob Marley. The dance floor was filled with couples having a great time and we quickly found ourselves doing the same.

Even though Carter was a terrible dancer, I found myself laughing more that night than any other night I could remember. Carter was a ball of energy so I could forgive him for all his really embarrassing NSYNC and Backstreet Boys moves.

No wonder no one bought his reggae album, I thought to myself with a giggle.

I tugged on his arm and shouted over the music, "I need to get some water. Let's take a break."

He nodded, grabbed my hand and we made our way off the dance floor.

"You looked great out there. I guess you never lost your touch in the dance department."

"I stayed up to date by watching YouTube and dancing around my house when Tom was at work and Meredith was at school."

"Sounds like a good use of time to me," he said nonjudgmentally as he reached for a bottle of water and handed one to me, as well.

"I probably should have been cleaning or cooking... you know, actually being productive at the time. No wonder I was such a crap housewife."

"Hey, remember the rule, no negative talk."

"Fine, fine," I said. "You were always annoyingly positive. Always being nice and trying to save the world."

He nodded. "That's me."

"I'm joking."

He looked at me and smiled. "I know. Someone had to be positive in our group. Piper always had her head in the clouds, you were always moping, so I was Mr. Optimistic by default."

He was right. Piper had been a little bit of a space cadet and I'd been a bit of a fatalist in college. Maybe that's why I'd married Tom. Maybe I thought I just couldn't do better.

Oh gosh, maybe I was still a fatalist and didn't know it. It was time to turn over a new leaf.

"Do you want to head home? You look a little tired."

"I do have to go to work early tomorrow," I said, feeling like a drag. I wanted to stay out and enjoy the nightlife, but I already found myself yawning. Clearly, I wasn't as young as I used to be.

"Come on, let's get you home. You're tired."

"No," I protested and then immediately yawned again. "I want to stay."

"One more dance and then I'm getting you home."

"Okay," I said as he again took my hand.

The evening was ending as the band switched from upbeat dance music to slow rhythms.

I wrapped my arms loosely around Carter's neck and he wrapped his around my waist and pulled me close. He was a great slow dancer.

I felt heat radiating between us. I was getting turned on feeling my breasts pressed against his body and so I snuggled up closer to him. He felt warm and inviting and I just wanted to stay in his arms forever.

"This is nice," I mumbled against his chest.

He grunted in reply, pulled me even closer and rested his chin on top of my head. He began to stroke my back and the motion was hypnotic as he rocked me to the beat of the music around the dance floor.

His sex was growing firm against me and I couldn't help but rub against it. But he was the perfect gentleman and pulled away just enough so that the evidence of his desire didn't press against me.

I wasn't a gentleman, and I leaned forward again, deliberately rubbing myself against his sex. He pulled his head back just enough to look down at me and said, "Keep doing that and I won't be able to control myself."

I arranged my smile into what I hoped was a contrite

expression and then naughtily pushed my hips against his.

He sucked in a breath and said, "I think we should get out of here."

"Good idea," I said, sounding breathless to my own ears.

He took my hand and led me to the car. Ours was one of the few that remained, and he didn't even wait to get inside the car before he roughly kissed me, pressing my back against the door as his lips possessively made their way across mine.

While we kissed, my hand made its way to his crotch and I began to rub against his hardness, changing my grip as I stroked him through the material of his pants.

His breath caught, and he bit my lower lip gently which made me gasp. He took advantage of that gasp to put his tongue in my mouth and I sucked on it gently, remembering the feel of his tongue between my legs, knowing how it felt to be penetrated by it.

I shivered at the memory, knowing I was growing wet.

"I want you," I murmured as he pulled his lips away and planted hot kisses near my ear and down my neck.

I couldn't help myself as I fumbled with his zipper to release his sex. He pulled away from my neck with a groan and stilled my hand with his own. "Not here," he said breathlessly.

He opened the car door and helped me in and then quickly climbed behind the wheel. As soon as he turned on the ignition, I snaked my hand between his legs and deftly released his sex.

I stroked him as he did his best to focus on driving us home. His cock was warm, long, and the tip was a little wet from pure lust.

I couldn't wait any longer, so when we paused at a red light, I lowered my mouth to his crotch and licked the drop of moisture I found there. He groaned, put the car in park and gripped my hair, keeping my head between his legs.

I sucked the tip of his cock into my mouth and then swallowed an inch more before releasing him slowly. I repeated the motion, taking in an inch of him at a time until I was able to get most of him in my mouth.

The car was silent other than his sighs. All we could hear was the noises I made as I sucked and licked his cock.

He became harder as I quickened the pace of my rhythm. His breath was rougher now, and I knew he was on the verge of coming.

I lightly trailed my teeth across his dick when a loud horn blasted behind us. Startled, I raised my head and Carter swore, put the car into drive and drove off.

I kept my hand on his dick, playing with it, rubbing it, keeping him hard. We didn't talk, didn't utter a sound and then before I knew it, we were at his place. As soon as he turned off the car, I was moving into his lap, positioning myself above his cock, ready to take him in.

He was more than ready for me and he slid his hands up my thighs, raising my mini-dress so that it gathered around my waist.

He placed his hands on my hips and I pulled my panties to the side and slowly lowered my waiting wetness onto his hard, pulsating, dick.

I moaned as I sheathed him fully inside me. I rode him hard. Greedily focusing only on reaching orgasm as quickly as possible. It didn't take long. As he filled me, and my sex greedily pulled at his cock, I was already beyond the point of no return. And within seconds I was coming, moaning his name as he played with my breasts and I began to grind against him over and over, trying to get him deeper as he came too, and I could feel his warm seed spill inside of me.

And as soon as it had started, it was over. And we stayed in that position, surrounded by the interior darkness of the car. Not a sound could be heard minus the panting of our own breaths as we sat there still connected. He lazily stroked my back and applied kisses to my shoulders and face. I lay against his shoulder and just breathed, moaning from time to time at the aftershocks that made my inner muscles clench around his cock in quick succession.

I could feel him growing hard again inside of me and so I began to move again, teasing his dick with each of my movements.

And so, we did it again and this time, I felt myself dozing as I nestled against his shoulders and reveled in the aftermath of our lovemaking.

He wrapped his arms around me and said gently, "Do you want to come inside?"

"I've come enough in one evening, thank you very much," I said with a sleepy yawn.

He laughed and stroked my back as I continued sitting in his lap, enjoying being connected to him. I felt our connection was more than physical. Being with Carter this way felt more than just sexual, it felt emotional. And finally, I understood what it felt like to be one with someone. His heartbeat echoed my own, his breaths were timed with mine. Our bodies and finally our hearts were on one accord.

Being with Carter was like being home. Carter was my home.

I slowly slid off him, immediately missing the feel of him inside me and the warmth of his arms.

"I would love to stay, but I have to get to work early tomorrow."

"What time?" he asked, stroking a hair out of my face.

"Seven."

"How about you spend the night and I'll wake you up at six?"

"You promise?"

He held up a hand as if he were a boy scout and said, "I promise."

I straightened my dress and he zipped up his pants. He then got out the car, walked to my side and opened the door for me.

He treated me like a lady when I certainly hadn't behaved like one and I adored him for it. He closed my door, held my hand and looked at me and smiled; I returned his smile. We didn't say anything, but there wasn't anything to be said.

Our bodies had done all the talking for us.

Feeling happier than I had in a long time, I let Carter lead me into his house, happily anticipating falling asleep in his arms.

$\mathcal{I}$ stretched gingerly and ignored the ache between my legs. Carter and I had made love most of the night and then again in the shower before I'd finally forced myself to go to work.

He had been a loving, sweet and caring lover, taking his time with me once I told him that I was a little sore from our shenanigans in his car.

Just thinking about our evening together gave me goosebumps and I could feel myself growing wet again as I lay in my cold bed alone, waiting for my alarm clock to go off.

I hadn't seen Carter in a week since he'd gone out of town to some sort of conference. I missed him so much.

I reached for my phone and texted him that. Almost instantaneously, I received a text in response that said, "Missing you too."

It made me smile and I had a feeling that if it could, my heart would be smiling too.

Humming, I made my way to the kitchen. Meredith surprised me. She was already up and when she saw me she gave me a big grin.

"Do you know what today is?"

I looked at her quizzically. "Hmmm let me think… let me think. I don't know… is today something special?"

"Mommmmmm," she said giving me a disappointed look. "It's a week before my birthday." She smiled up at me and said, "Sooooo what do you have planned?"

I couldn't help but laugh. "If I tell you then it wouldn't be a surprise."

Her eyes widened, and she clapped her hands excitedly. "I knew it! I knew it! A surprise party!"

She hugged me around my waist and squeezed tightly. "Thank you thank you thank you. It's going to be the best surprise party ever."

I realized then that maybe she didn't get the whole concept of what a surprise party was meant to be, but she was only five and I didn't want to burst her bubble.

"Get ready for school, we don't want you to be late."

She skipped off humming, but then she turned around quickly and said, "Mom… um… you did invite Daddy and Becca to my party, right?"

I nodded. "Of course, sweetheart. Daddy and I love you very much. Of course he'll be there."

"And Becca too?"

I wanted to sigh but repressed it. Becca, for all her sweetness, was still not my favorite person. I knew that I was just jealous of her because she was nineteen, skinny, and beautiful. I felt petty, but she was Miss Perfect while I was Miss Kind of Good Enough.

"I'm sure Becca wouldn't miss your party. She loves you too much to miss it. You're like her number one person."

Meredith beamed and then suddenly ran to me and gave me another big hug. "You're the best mom. Danny Schultz's mom won't even let him see his dad. She's crazy."

I shook my head. Danny Schultz had lots of stories to tell. I was glad Meredith wasn't exchanging crazy mom stories with him. Yikes.

"Well, that's too bad. I'm sure Danny misses his dad."

"I think he's in prison. I think he robbed a bank."

"Well that explains why she drives that fancy car and can afford private school," I said to myself and then instantly remembered that kids repeated EVERY-THING. "Honey, please don't repeat what mommy just said. It wasn't nice."

She looked confused but just shrugged it off. "Okay. I don't know what you're talking about anyway."

The conversation already forgotten, she skipped to her room and shut the door behind her.

I dropped Meredith off at school and was pleased to see Carter there. He was in a deep discussion with the woman whose car I'd hit. When she saw me, she gave me a little wave. I guess she was done hating me.

Carter excused himself and made his way to the drop-off line and stopped at my car.

"You have plans for this weekend?" he asked.

I smiled and shrugged flirtatiously. "Maybe… depends on who's asking." And then I immediately stiffened up, I did have plans for the weekend. I was such a dope.

"I mean, I actually do have plans. It's Meredith's birthday this weekend. We're throwing her a surprise party at Piper's house."

Piper and I had patched things up pretty easily. We both hated to be mad at each other so after a few "I'm sorry's" and a few tears, we were right back to being tight friends. She had offered to host Meredith's party at her house months ago. At the time, I'd been barely speaking to Tom, so Piper's house had been considered "neutral" territory.

"Oh, she'll love that."

I nodded, "She's excited about it already, so it won't be much of a surprise." I brushed my bangs away from my face. "You should come. I'm sure Meredith would love to see you there."

He nodded. "It's a deal. I'll see you then."

He made his way back up the front steps and into the school and I found myself thinking about how sexy he walked. I was caught off-guard by my thought process. It seemed now every time I thought of Carter the word sexy popped up in my head.

Like lovesick teenagers, we called each other every day. We talked about nothing important, but I frequently fell asleep with my phone next to my ear, drifting off after we'd talked for hours on end. Sometimes it was almost daybreak before we got off the phone.

I learned a lot about his life over the years. It turns out that his stepmother had opened a thriving family law practice not too long ago. I remember her being a no-nonsense woman who freely spoke her mind. I hadn't known that she was a lawyer. If I'd known that I wouldn't have used the last bit of savings to take Tom to court over shared custody on an incompetent lawyer that rarely returned my phone calls.

Besides that, I also realized that Carter was probably the most giving person I'd met in my life. I already knew that in college, but he hadn't changed one bit. He'd spent time in Suriname working with an indigenous population there. He'd also traveled throughout Brazil, working with teachers and students there to implement technological changes in the schools.

And most recently, he'd been a principal of a small international school in Guatemala. I was in awe of him. He'd done so much and had positively impacted so many lives. He literally had made the world a better place. I was proud of him even though I'd always known that was the type of person he was.

I found myself opening up to him about a lot of things in my marriage that I hadn't shared with anyone, not even Piper.

I talked about how I felt like I'd just been going through the motions when I was married. I talked to him about how I thought I might have been depressed because some days, especially the days before I was pregnant with Meredith, I'd been so unhappy I hadn't even bothered to get out of bed.

And Tom had never noticed. Or maybe he had and just didn't care enough to say anything about it.

One thing was for certain, Carter cared. He wanted to know everything about my life over the past few years, the good and the bad. He asked me about my relationship with my parents and if they were still the same. Sadly, I'd informed him that they hadn't changed a bit and their example of parenting informed mine—I knew exactly how NOT to raise Meredith.

We covered so many topics— from our disappointments to our proud moments over the years and it was nice to have someone to reflect with. Carter was a great listener. A great lover. A great friend.

He was everything my ex hadn't been. And so I was glad that Carter had chosen to fall in love with me. I'm sure he'd met plenty of women over the years that he could have built a life with, but he hadn't. And part of me wanted to believe he'd been waiting for me. I knew that was a fairytale ideal, but the romantic in me, who I rarely let surface, loved to believe in the impossible.

Speaking of love, we hadn't said the "L" word to each other. I thought maybe it would be premature to do so, but honestly, it would be late. Carter had been more than just my college crush. I just hadn't admitted it. I'd loved him from afar all throughout college, I just thought that love and happiness were a thing of fairy tales. At least, that was what my parents had always led me to believe.

I realized now that I'd been modeling their relationship. My mom had married an emotionless, absent man and I'd done the same. I'd repeated her mistake. I figured now was the time to stop making the mistakes of others and learn to make mistakes of my own. That way, at least I could own up to it and accept that I'd made a choice even if that choice was wrong.

The week passed by faster than I expected and the next thing I knew it was the day of the party. I'd solicited Piper's help and to my surprise, Becca also joined us.

I was determined to be nice to her. She treated Meredith like her long-lost daughter and made her laugh, I couldn't ask for anything more.

"Thanks for letting me help out," she said to me as she helped hang the streamers while Piper ran out to collect the cakes and cupcakes that I'd ordered.

I fought with a streamer that had gotten tangled around my arms while saying, "No, thank you for offering to help. Clearly, I need it." I gave the streamer one firm tug and it promptly fell from the ceiling, undoing about twenty minutes of hard work.

"Ugghhh..." I said, pressing my palm against my forehead in frustration.

Becca laughed and jumped down from the chair she had been standing on. "I got it."

We worked in silence, fixing what I'd messed up until finally it was done.

"Not too bad," I said, looking around at our work.

"You don't think there's too much pink, do you?"

I pretended to be in deep consideration as I said, "There can never be too much pink."

She smiled at me and then her face grew serious. "Umm... Dana? I just want to clear the air..." she cleared her throat nervously.

I looked at her in concern. Clear the air? What was she talking about? I stared at her for a second, trying to guess what was coming next, but wanting to just run away and hide. Was she going to tell me off or something? I'd thought I'd been nice the whole time, but who knew? "You okay? Everything alright? Did I do something to upset you?"

She nodded, then thought better of it and said, "Well no. I mean… it has nothing to do with you."

Now I was curious. "What's wrong Becca?"

"I just want you to know that I was not seeing Tom while you guys were married. I would never ever do that. I swear to God."

I raised my brows. I didn't know where this confession was coming from.

"You do believe me, don't you?" she asked me, looking as if she were about to cry.

"Becca, me and Tom are old news, if you were seeing him while we were married—"

"I wasn't! I swear I wasn't!" she cried, tears welling in her eyes.

I felt instantly terrible. "Hey, don't cry! I was just going to say that I'd moved on. That part of my life is over. I don't care what Tom does or did."

She sighed. "Thank you. That means a lot. I just didn't want you to think I was some conniving whore."

That's exactly what I'd thought she was, before I'd

gotten to know her, but there was no way I was going to tell her that.

"I don't think ill of you, Becca. I really don't"

She stared at me and narrowed her eyes. "Are you sure?"

"Very."

"Good. Because I'm leaving Tom. And I wanted you to be the first to know."

I stared at her in shock and said the first thing that popped into my head. "But you guys have only been married for like a minute!"

"One minute too long," she said, swiping at tears. "I just don't think I love him. And I don't think he loves me. Call me silly, but I'm only nineteen. I don't want to be tied down the rest of my life to someone who doesn't love me only to wake up seven years later and watch him divorce me and marry someone half my age..."

"Ummm... that's exactly what he did to me."

"I know!" she said, "I can't let that be my future. I'm not stupid... I know you think I am—"

"I don't think you're stupid, Becca," I said fiercely. Now I felt terrible for thinking anything bad about her. Clearly, she was hurting.

"Well, I'm not stupid. A little naïve, but not stupid. The only reason I even stuck around past a month was because Meredith is such a sweetheart and I know what it feels like to grow up in a home shuttled between parents. I just wanted to be her friend, you know? And now I feel terrible that I'm leaving her and her father."

She started sobbing then and I reached out to put my arms around her. She was smarter than I'd given her credit for. She was also clearly a beautiful person.

"Listen to me, don't you feel bad for an instant about leaving Tom. And don't stay with him a minute longer out of a sense of guilt. Meredith is a trooper. She'll adjust. Trust me. That's why I stayed so long and stayed so miserable. I thought I was doing what was right but I wasn't. What was right would have been showing Meredith what a functional relationship looks like. And Tom and I were anything but functional."

Becca continued to cry, and I awkwardly tried to soothe her. "It's fine… you'll be fine. Stop crying," I pleaded.

"But," she said, trying to compose herself as she pulled away and reached for her bag. She started to fix her makeup. "Will you still let me see Meredith after Tom and I divorce? I know he won't, but I thought that maybe you would? I don't want to stop being a part of her life."

And I know Meredith would have felt the same way. She went on and on about all the fun things she and Becca would do together. She loved Becca and there was no way I was going to hurt the special relationship they had.

"Becca, I promise you can see Meredith whenever you want. She loves you and I wouldn't do anything to jeopardize your relationship with her." I paused then and asked, "You said I was the first to know. Does that mean Tom doesn't even know yet?"

She shook her head. "I was going to wait until tonight after the party. Since it's your weekend, I figured it would be better to do it now so that Meredith wouldn't hear us argue. My parents argued all the time and it was a nightmare." She shook her head. "I already packed a bag."

"Where will you go?" I said.

"Oh, to my dad's… he doesn't live far from here. He never liked Tom anyway."

"Okay. This is awkward, saying this to my husband's soon to be ex who technically replaced me, but if you need anything we're here for you."

She embraced me tightly in another big hug. "Thank you sooo much. That means so much to me."

I pried myself from her embrace and murmured an excuse about needing to pick up some additional things.

My mind was running everywhere. I couldn't believe what I'd just heard. I wanted to immediately tell Piper but I didn't even know where she was.

I got in the car to pick up the remaining things. Becca offered to come with me, so we went together.

I got to know her pretty well in the thirty minutes

that we were in the car together and I felt bad that I hadn't made an effort to get to know her sooner. But she was married to my ex-husband, so I didn't beat myself up too badly about it.

"So where were you raised, Becca?"

"I'm from here. Born and raised. I haven't ever lived anywhere else, but my mom and my other siblings live in Oregon. I'm the oldest. I stayed with my dad after they got divorced."

"I was raised here too, well about forty minutes from here."

"Oh? Do you have family still here?"

"My mom and Dad."

She looked surprised. "Oh, Meredith never mentions her grandparents."

I instantly felt bad. "Yeah, my parents are pretty hands-off. They're not very involved in Meredith's life, unfortunately. They send birthday cards when they remember."

"Are they coming to Becca's party?"

I shrugged. "Who knows?"

Becca frowned. "I hate to judge, but what kind of people can't make the time to come to their own granddaughter's birthday party? I know they're your parents but that's kind of harsh."

I nodded because she was right. "My parents are in a league of their own, that's for sure."

We talked about her dreams and aspirations and I realized that Becca was really smart and motivated. I liked her.

"So how are things going with you and Carter?"

I figured that it wouldn't hurt to tell her.

"Things are going really well." I paused and then said, "I always had a crush on him. We were best friends. We met in college—"

"What? But didn't you marry Tom right after college?"

"Yeah, but—"

"Carter was your one true love?"

I laughed, and I was about to brush off her comment when it hit me. "Yeah," I said to her, "I think that's exactly it."

"That's so romantic," she said. "That's what I want. I want to love someone who will love me more than a year. Like forever would be nice."

I laughed. "Yeah, that's the goal. I wish I'd figured that out a long time ago. If I had I wouldn't be the product of a messy divorce."

Becca grew silent. "Do you think our divorce will be messy?"

I'd already forgotten that Becca was about to be former wife number two.

"Well, it's different for you. You're getting out before

things get complicated. You know, before you have kids."

"Oh well, that part was a given. Tom doesn't want any more kids."

She sounded sad.

"You want kids one day?"

She nodded. "Yeah, I want a ton of kids."

"What's a ton?"

"Like five."

I laughed hard. "Five? Wow."

Becca smiled. "I grew up with a ton of younger siblings so I'd be so bored with just one. I want a bunch of kids so that none of them are lonely."

"Becca, you really are a sweetheart."

"I swear I'm not an evil stepmother."

"Well, Tom is sure losing a jewel."

She smiled at me. "That's so nice of you to say."

"I mean it. And I'm glad you're going to stick around in Meredith's life."

"And I'm glad you found love with someone else," she said as we pulled up to Piper's house. And as we did, the subject of our most recent comment popped up.

Carter stepped out of his car and pulled out a few bags and then waved at me as best as he could.

"Hey there! I brought a few more things to eat. I figured you can't have too much."

He then walked up and kissed me on the cheek. Upon seeing Becca, he smiled at her. "Becca, right?"

She nodded. "You remembered."

"Of course, I do. Meredith speaks of you very fondly."

She practically glowed at his compliment.

"You're definitely a keeper," she said to Carter. "Definitely an upgrade from Tom," she said before excusing herself and heading back into the house.

"Hmmm, what was that comment about?" Carter said looking confused. "Trouble in paradise?"

"She's planning to leave Tom."

His eyes widened. "Really? They haven't even been married a year, right?"

"Apparently she's a smart woman who knows her worth."

"But still a shocker. Does Tom know yet?"

"Nope. She's telling him tonight."

"Yikes. This is your weekend with Meredith, right? So she won't be there when Tom's world implodes around him."

"Yep it's my weekend, but Tom is going to be pissed. Totally blindsided, I bet. So yeah, he'll pretty much feel exactly like I did."

Carter shrugged indifferently. "Sucks to be him."

We didn't get a chance to talk more about it because the party quickly started. About twenty students from

Meredith's class showed up and some of them brought siblings. I was grateful that Carter had thought to bring more food. I even got to meet the infamous Danny Schultz and his mom. I was starting to think that maybe Meredith had a crush on Danny. She grabbed him by the hand as soon as he arrived and made him shake all the gifts with her as they attempted to guess what was inside each box.

Tom showed up in the middle of the party, but I noticed Becca attempted to keep her distance. Whenever he was on one side of the room, she was on the other. I knew he was pissed about it and I could see the frown on his face. Tom wasn't a yeller. He liked to tear you down with targeted insults and the silent treatment. And I knew he wouldn't make a scene at the party, but I knew it was clear as day that Becca was avoiding being near him.

What I'd thought was going to be a pretty low-key party turned into quite a huge affair. To my surprise, my parents did show up. They murmured something about being in town. I ignored the fact they were always in town and lived only fifteen minutes away from where we currently lived because I was just happy that they showed up at all. I always invited them, but they rarely showed up to any event concerning Meredith.

Carter was surprised to see them as well.

"Wow, I think that's only the second time I've seen them since we've known each other."

"Yep," I said. "That's probably the second time Meredith has seen them in like her whole life."

"They're still a piece of work."

I sighed and nodded. "I don't miss being married to Tom but I do miss his mom. She had been really kind and motherly. I wish Meredith had gotten the chance to meet her."

Carter nodded. "She was a sweet lady. Piper took her death pretty hard."

"Between you and me, I think that was the reason Piper stayed away from home so long. I think she just didn't want to deal with the pain of losing her."

"That's something I understand all too well."

He wrapped an arm around my shoulder and I reached for his hand. I felt that he was talking about me. But I didn't want to be presumptuous. I missed him though. I realized that now. I'd been unhappy because I'd been so alone. Tom had worked all the time and emotionally checked out of our marriage early. I'd done the same. I'm not sure why we'd married each other. We'd both clearly been unhappy.

Carter went off to go supervise the kids in the bouncy house in the back that I'd rented. Piper had been in charge of the bouncy house at first, but she had invited her magician boyfriend to the party so her attention had been torn. I guess now they were official. She had abandoned the bouncy house to perform some tricks for the children, so she was acting as her boyfriend's trusty magician assistant. She even had her own uniform. She looked like she was having the best time.

The end of the night was approaching and slowly the students began to go home. The parents thanked me, and Meredith was a gracious host, happily saying goodbye to all our guests before breaking down and letting out a sleepy yawn.

It wasn't even seven o'clock, but we were all tired.

I had Piper take Meredith to her room for a nap while Carter helped me clean up. Tom looked on angrily. Eventually, he approached me and asked me if he could talk to me in private for a second.

Carter looked concerned but didn't interfere.

When we were out of earshot, Tom said, "I really would appreciate if you wouldn't flaunt your relationship with a man you're not even married to while Meredith is over here. I'm trying to raise her with morals and watching her mom slut it up with a school administrator doesn't make a good impression."

I was instantly livid.

"Slutting it up? First of all, you have no right to judge me. You married a teenager, Tom. Before the ink was even fresh on our divorce paperwork you were already screwing someone else, so save your judgment."

He didn't even blink. "Is he sleeping over at your house?"

"What I do in my own home is none of your business."

"It is my business when my daughter is involved."

"You really have some nerve, Tom, trying to tell me how to live my life as if you're some sort of paragon of virtue."

"You're no mother Teresa yourself," he snapped back. "If I find out that asshole is staying over, I swear there will be hell to pay."

"The only asshole here is you. And once again, you don't tell me how to live my life or what to do. I'm not your wife anymore. You couldn't control what I said and did then, you must be crazy if you think you can control me now. And instead of worrying about what's happening in my relationship, maybe you should worry about your own."

I felt I'd already said too much and instantly wanted to backtrack. I didn't want him to think I'd influenced Becca's decision. And I knew Tom too well. He always needed someone to blame and I wasn't interested in being his scapegoat anymore.

Not wanting to say more, I tried to walk away before he could get in another word.

He caught me by my elbow and then I heard a voice say behind me, "Everything okay, Dana?"

It was Carter.

"Go mind your business, Carter. Dana and I are discussing things that don't require your input. Not that it would be welcomed anyway."

"I'm sure whatever you have to say to Dana can wait. Tonight is about Meredith and the last thing she needs right now is for her father to make a scene."

Tom looked at Carter with hatred.

"You think you've won. Don't you?" We all knew what Tom was talking about. He hated the idea of Carter and I being together. That was no secret.

"Dana was never a prize, Tom. She's a person and it's about time you start treating and respecting her like one."

"Who the hell do you think you are? You think you can tell me what to do? You're nobody to me." He took a threatening step towards Carter.

"Tom—" I said, not wanting things to escalate.

Carter didn't take his eyes off Tom. "Go ahead. Try it," he said, stepping up to Tom until their faces were inches away.

"Still can't get over the fact that you were the loser, can you? After all these years, I bet it eats you up that she chose me over you. But what did you expect? You were some dirty, hippie wannabe when what she wanted was a real man."

"Stop talking, Tom. You're embarrassing yourself," Piper said, appearing out of nowhere as she pushed Tom back, stepping in between the two guys who would have been at each other's throats by now. "You're such a prima donna. Everything has to be about you. It's like you go out of your way to ruin other people's happiness. We get it, dude. You think you're special. But you're not. You're just like the rest of us—"

He laughed. "Like the rest of you? Piper, you're dating a magician. Carter is a principal. How much does that pay? A whopping sixty thou a year? I make that in three months. And seriously, Dana. I traded up. I mean have you seen how hot Becca is? She's not some broken down, overweight housewife."

I flinched. "Get out."

He opened his mouth to say something but then his eyes trained on something behind us. Becca stood there with a disgusted look on her face.

She didn't even acknowledge Tom as she turned towards us. "Piper, Dana, thanks for having me over. I really appreciate it. And for what it's worth, I think you guys are amazing."

She turned and walked away. Tom scampered behind her and tried to take her hand. She pushed him away and stomped to the car. Words were exchanged, but I couldn't tell what was being said. And then they were gone.

My mom and dad, who I hadn't noticed before, stood there silently. Clearly, they had overheard the drama.

"I never liked that man," my dad said suddenly, and my mom nodded in agreement.

I looked at them annoyed. "A few months ago, you guys were saying that I needed to work to get him back."

"That was before you proved you could take care of yourself," my mom said.

Coming from my parents, that was a huge compliment. Even if it was sort of a backhanded comment.

Then my mom added, "I thought you and Meredith were going to end up on welfare for sure, but you proved me wrong."

Just when I thought my parents could be kind of warm, of course, she said something like that. Of course.

"Thanks for the vote of confidence."

"Sure thing," my dad said, clueless to my sarcasm. "We're leaving now. Be sure you buy Meredith a decent pair of shoes with the gift card we gave her. Her shoes looked old and dusty."

"It makes you look poor, dear," my mom said for good measure.

"Well, I definitely wouldn't want to look poor... even though, technically I am, but thanks for that, Mom."

She gave me a tight smile and said, "If you keep a job

you'll be out of poverty in no time. In the meantime, at least try not to get into public fights with your ex-husband. It's kind of unbecoming." She turned to my dad. "I want to be home before my show."

He nodded, gave everyone a cold wave and disappeared with my mom through the door.

Piper and Carter looked at me with a mixture of shock and pity on their faces.

"I'm not sure what was worse, Tom's tirade or my parents' crazy backhanded compliments."

Piper shook her head. "I think it's a tie."

We went back to cleaning up the house. Piper chatted happily, but Carter and I barely said a word. It seemed both of us were deep in thought.

When Piper walked away to take a call from a client, I finally opened up.

"Thanks for sticking up for me."

Carter shrugged it off. "Tom has always been an idiot."

"I don't know what I ever saw in him."

"Well, it doesn't matter now. He's old news."

"And you're my present," I said, reaching out for his hand. He took it and brought it to his lips.

"And maybe your future?" he asked, pulling me into his arms.

"I think I could get used to that," I said as he lowered

his lips to mine. It was a soft, gentle kiss and as I pulled away, I heard a distinctive giggle.

I turned in the direction of the door and guiltily pulled myself out of Carter's arms.

"Hey, you, when did you wake up?" I said, trying to appear nonchalant as Meredith looked from me to Carter.

"I saw you two kissing." Her tone was mocking.

"Well, we—"

"Uhhh—"

Meredith sighed. "You can kiss Principal K all you want Mommy. It's a free country."

And then she just turned around and walked away. I looked at Carter and he looked at me and shrugged.

"Should we continue from where we left off?"

I gave him a look and he instantly looked contrite. "Well, it is a free country."

I couldn't help myself. I leaned forward and kissed him, catching him off-guard.

It felt amazing to be so in love.

9

I sat in front of my computer screen, not really seeing what was on the monitor. My mind was elsewhere. I felt like a lovesick teenager. I couldn't stop thinking of Carter. We'd gone on a couple's retreat for the weekend and I'd had the chance to meet some of his friends.

A few months had passed since Meredith's birthday party and it seemed that Becca had reconsidered the whole leaving Tom idea. I hadn't gotten a chance to talk to her because she no longer answered her phone and Meredith told me she'd gotten a job.

I had a sneaky suspicion that maybe Becca was just trying to get her ducks in a row before she decided to up and leave Tom. At least, I hoped that's what her plan was. She definitely deserved more than Tom, just like I'd deserved more.

The few short months Carter and I had been together really contrasted with the type of relationship I'd had with Tom. Tom and I had never been laidback or fun. I'd spent most of my time just trying to prove that I deserved to be with him. I'd been devoted and stupid.

Even when I was miserable, I'd still blamed myself. I told myself that I should have been happy, that a million women would love to have my life. I'd been fooling myself. I'd been miserable married to Tom, but too stubborn and pitiful to just quit living a lie.

My boss walked by at that moment and touched my shoulder. She was the nicest person. She was the opposite of Mr. Baxter and I was happy that I was finally full-time with the company. Not only that, I'd technically been promoted and I was now their social media strategist. I guess all I'd needed was a little exposure and now all of a sudden, I was an expert. And my paycheck reflected it. It was exciting to be able to buy things for Meredith. We'd probably gone on a bit too many impromptu shopping trips since my income increased.

"Isn't it time for you to pick up your daughter?"

I looked at the time and swore softly. It was an early drop-off today, Becca had insisted on it which was unusual. Normally, she always asked for more time.

I waved goodbye to my colleagues and walked quickly to my car. I planned to meet Becca at the grocery store near my home. I arrived just in time to see her arrive. She pulled up in her little Mercedes and Meredith hopped out.

She happily walked to me and gave me a big hug. "See you later, Becca!" She climbed into the car as Becca said to me, "Can I talk to you?"

"Sure, what's up?" I said stepping out of the car and out of earshot.

"I'm going to do it tonight. I chickened out before. But I'm going to do it. I have a new job and now I can support myself instead of living off my dad which was my original plan."

"Oh yeah, how's the job going?"

"Oh, it's great! It's at the local community college, so I get to work in the bookstore and go to school at the same time. I start next semester. I'm kind of nervous but excited too."

"Great, that's really great, Becca."

"So anyway, that's why I wanted to drop Meredith off a little early. I didn't want her home for when Tom found the note."

My mouth fell open. "You left him a note?"

"Oh yeah. I hate confrontation." She shrugged. "I'm sure it's fine."

I didn't know what to say so I just gave her a nod and wished her good luck.

"Meredith doesn't know yet, does she?"

Becca looked sad. "I didn't know how to tell her. So I kind of just wrote her a note too."

"What!" I shrieked. "You didn't give it to her yet, did you?"

"Nooooo," Becca said as if I were stupid. She reached into her pocket and said, "I hoped that you would?"

She handed me the piece of paper and I groaned to myself. Why was Becca making me do the hard part?

As if reading my mind, she said, "I'm sorry that I'm making you do the hard part, but I just can't."

And then she started crying and I stood in front of her and desperately begged her to stop. "Stop crying unless you want to explain to Meredith right now what's going on."

Becca continued crying. I peeked over my shoulder and said, "If she sees you crying, she'll know something's up and then things will REALLY get awkward."

"Okay, okay," Becca said, sniffling.

I awkwardly reached out and hugged her. She held me like she was going to break and then said, "Thanks for everything."

I gave her a stiff smile and got back into the car.

"What's wrong with Becca?" Meredith asked.

I sighed. "Honey, you know how much we love you, right? But sometimes adults just don't get along—"

"No!" she screamed. "Don't tell me you're breaking up with Principal K!"

"What? No!"

She sighed. "That's a relief. He's a nice guy. A real keeper. That's what Auntie Piper calls him. And plus, he's your friend. You shouldn't break up with your friend."

"Well, I don't plan to."

"That would be a tragedy."

I laughed at how dramatic she sounded. And then I remembered that I was trying to discuss a serious matter with her.

"Well, I know this will be hard for you to understand honey, and understand this has nothing to do with you, but Becca has decided that she wants to do something different in her life."

"Oh? Is she going back to college? She should. She's really smart."

"Um… maybe, but by different, I mean I don't think she wants to be married anymore."

To my surprise, Meredith sighed deeply. "I'm not surprised," she said in a rather adult tone. "Becca is like half his age! Danny already told me that his mom said it would never work out."

I opened my mouth. Then closed it and then opened it again. "I got nothing," I said.

"Mom, sometimes adults don't get along and they part ways. It's no one's fault."

Hadn't I just told her that? "Well, that's very mature

of you, but if you feel sad and you want to talk about it, you just let me know, okay?"

She nodded and then said a few minutes later, "Does this mean I don't get to see Becca anymore? I don't think Daddy will let me see her since he'll be mad at her, you know?"

"Well, I don't know what your dad plans to do, but I know how much you love Becca and I know how much she loves you, so if you still want to spend time with her that's perfectly fine with me."

"I would like that," she said softly. "She's my friend."

"I know she is, hon." I reached for the note when I pulled up to a stoplight and scanned it quickly.

I handed it to Meredith.

"What's this?"

"A note from Becca to you."

She read the letter as we drove home.

"You okay?" I asked as we pulled up to the house.

She nodded, and I went to the back to help her out of her car seat. She got out without a word and I sensed that all wasn't well. I sighed. I hated Tom for all Meredith had gone through.

"What would you like for dinner?" I asked, trying to keep things normal.

She didn't answer, instead, she ran to me and wrapped her arms around me and cried. I held her and stroked her hair.

"It's okay, hon. I promise you, everything will be fine." I hated the pain that Tom and Becca's break up was already causing her. "I promise you, hon, that no matter what, everything will be okay. I love you."

She sniffled, gave me a watery smile and said, "I love you too, Mom."

I would do anything to protect Meredith, but I knew as she held me tightly and continued to cry that some pain I couldn't spare her. And with tears in my eyes, I promised to myself that I would do anything in my power to never make her cry.

10

<hr>

My phone was ringing. I only realized that after I fell out of my bed blindly reaching for it. I couldn't tell the time, but I knew it was before seven since the sun was just starting to rise.

"Hello?" I said sleepily.

"You bitch."

"What?" I said pulling the phone away from my ear and looking at the number. It was my ex.

"You think you won, don't you? You filled Becca's head with bullshit and now she's gone."

I was now wide awake. "If Becca decided to leave you, that had nothing to do with me. Trust me, you're reason enough to send any woman running for her life. Goodbye."

I hung up the phone and shook my head. I guess he'd read her note.

I was in a deep sleep when I heard the banging on my door.

I jumped up to answer it when a sleepy Meredith appeared in the hallway. "Who's that, Mom?"

I pushed her back towards her room and said, "You go lie back down. I'll check it out."

"Who's there?" I called, tightening my robe that I'd grabbed at the last minute since I preferred to only wear a t-shirt to bed.

No one responded so I looked through the peephole and saw Tom standing there. He didn't look so good. He looked like he'd barely slept.

I opened the door a little and immediately went on the offensive. "What are you doing here, Tom? What do you want?"

"I'm here for my daughter."

"What?"

"You heard me."

"This is my weekend, not yours. Per our custody agreement, you'll get her when it's your time."

I tried to close the door when he grabbed the side of it, keeping me from shutting it firmly in his face.

"Is that asshole Carter here?"

"That's none of your business."

He shook his head. "None of my business? You convince my wife to leave me, yet you're messing around with Carter is none of my business?"

I looked behind me and could see no sign of Meredith peeking around the corner, but that didn't mean that she wasn't somewhere eavesdropping.

"My relationship with Carter is not up for discussion."

"The hell it isn't."

"Get off my property. Now."

"Not without my daughter."

"She's not leaving this house until I say so. You can threaten, scream at me, insult me. I don't care. But unless you have a court order or police escort, my daughter will not leave this house unless I say so."

He was so angry his face started to turn red. "Who do you think you are?"

"A pissed off mom who is about to slam your hand in this door."

"You wouldn't—"

"Try me." My voice was cold, my eyes were too. I guess he saw the look on my face because he instantly removed his hand.

"I'm going to take you to court. And you know what, Dana? I'm going to win. Look at you and look at me. I was being nice to you giving you 50/50 custody, but no more mister nice guy. You don't deserve it. I'm not going to have you filling my daughter's head with lies like you filled my wife's."

"For the last time, I had nothing to do with Becca

leaving you." My voice was shaky. "But I don't blame her. I wish I'd come to my senses and done the same."

"I wish you had too. If it weren't for Meredith, I would easily chalk our marriage up to be the worst decision of my life."

My face flushed with anger and I growled, "Funny. I'm sure Becca would say the same thing about you."

It was his turn to turn red. He seemed ready to blow a gasket. But then Meredith peeked out the door from around me and looked up at Tom. "Daddy, what are you doing here? And why are you yelling at Mom?"

He took a step back and composed himself. "I just missed you, sweetheart, that's all. I just wanted to check to make sure you were okay. I'll come get you tomorrow, okay? We'll go to the zoo."

I looked down at her. "Go on back to bed. I need to speak to your father in private."

She looked between the two of us and then made her way back to her bedroom. I didn't want to risk her overhearing us, so I stepped out of my drafty house in my bathrobe and faced my ex.

"I don't know what you think I told Becca but I assure you her decision to leave you was all hers. I've had nothing to do with it. Becca loves Meredith and it tore her up to make the decision to leave her."

Tom's eyes narrowed. "So you did talk to her about this?"

"Only with regards to Meredith—"

"That's all I needed to know. I'll see you in court."

He didn't say another word. He just walked away. My heart was racing, my palms were damp, and I was already tearing up. I took a deep breath and wiped away the tear that had escaped. I was strong. I wouldn't let him threaten me, I told myself and then tried to muster some composure before I went back inside where I knew Meredith would be sitting eagerly waiting for me.

I opened the door, locked it behind me and then looked into my living room. To my surprise, Meredith wasn't there.

She was in her room. I thought she went back to sleep, but then I could see her eyes were open and she was staring blankly at the ceiling.

"You okay?" I asked.

"I'm fine."

"Okay, if you want to talk—"

"Is Daddy going to take me away from you because Becca left?"

"No, honey, no," I said, crossing over and sitting down next to her on the bed. I took her in my arms and she seemed to be shaking.

I realized then that she was holding back tears. "Daddy is just angry. He'll be fine. Everything will be fine, you'll see."

"I don't want him to take me away from you," she

said, her voice catching on a sob. And just like that, she started to cry, hard. Her tears ran freely, and I held her tighter and didn't know I was crying too until my tears dampened her hair.

I swiped at my tears and made her turn around and face me. "That's not going to happen. Do you hear me? I'm not going to let your daddy take you away from me. I'm still going to see you every Wednesday and every other weekend."

She didn't look convinced. "Daddy's rich and power-ful… we're kind of poor and well, kind of poor—"

It saddened me that she already knew how this world worked.

"I'll use every drop of money I have to be sure it never comes to that. I promise you, Meredith, your daddy will not take you away from me. Not in a million years."

She seemed reassured then and laid her head on my chest. I rocked her back and forth like I'd done when she was a toddler and she drifted back to sleep.

I'd spoke with absolute certainty but now I was unsure. Was Tom bluffing or was he really going to try to ruin my life over a broken marriage that was entirely his fault?

* * *

TWO WEEKS LATER, I'd all but forgotten my confrontation with Tom. He had sent the maid out to pick Meredith up from our designated drop-off place and so I hadn't seen him. I'd been both relieved and apprehensive. He always met me at the drop-off unless Becca volunteered.

I told myself that I needn't be worried. And when my weekend rolled around, I went to the drop-off station and waited intently.

When he was ten minutes late, I picked up my phone and called him. It went straight to voicemail. By thirty minutes, I was starting to worry. I called three more times. I sat there for an hour fretting and nervous when finally he pulled up.

I sucked in a breath of relief.

"Where were you? You could have at least told me you planned to be late," I said as he got out the car. Something was wrong. There was no sign of Meredith. Where was Meredith?

I looked at him sharply. "Where's Meredith?

"She's home," he said, leaning against his car and folding his arms.

"What do you mean she's home? Why isn't she here with you?'

"Well, it doesn't take a genius to figure that out. I'm not dropping her off."

"What?"

"You heard me."

"You're in violation of the court order—"

"I'm getting the court order redone and until then Meredith will be staying with me."

"You can't do that. You can't withhold my visitation rights!" I said and noticed the tears running down my face when I felt something salty in my mouth. My breathing was uneven and it took all my inner will to not punch him in his throat.

He must have realized that I was ready to explode because his eyes were cold and his tone was full of mockery and derision as he said, "What are you going to do? Call the cops? Take me back to court? We both know you wouldn't call the cops and end up upsetting Meredith and you're too broke to take me to court."

"Bring my daughter to me."

"No. I just came to tell you to keep your eye on your mail. I want the custody order revisited and I intend to fight you until that happens."

I lost my temper and slammed my hand down so hard on the ceiling of his car, that I left a dent.

He didn't even flinch. "I'm sure the court will love to hear about how you damaged my personal property out of spite."

"Why are you doing this, Tom? What do you want?"

"Primary custody with all your visitations supervised."

I felt as if someone had knocked the breath out of me. At that moment, I hated Tom with every fiber of my being. "You're an asshole and I hope you burn in hell," I growled, meaning every word.

I received derisive laughter in response.

"There's no way I'm going to let you have primary custody. And there's no way I'm doing supervised visits."

"Fine. Then I guess you won't be seeing Meredith."

"Bring my daughter home."

"She is home," he said nastily.

"Look, Tom. You're angry with me for whatever reason, but it doesn't have to be this way."

"It doesn't feel good, does it, Dana? When someone takes away the person you love?"

I closed my eyes and shuddered. "I told you I didn't have anything to do with Becca's decision."

"Doesn't matter now. I'll tell you what," he said with an evil chuckle. "I'm willing to drop the whole primary custody thing."

"What's the catch?" I whispered. There was always a catch with Tom.

"You stop seeing Carter."

"You can't tell me who I can or cannot date."

"An eye for an eye. You took away my Becca and I'm going to make sure you and your dear Carter can't be together. So those are my terms. If you don't want me to set my lawyer on you then you do that one simple thing." He added, "And don't try to sneak around with him behind my back. I would find out. So what do you think of my terms?"

I turned away from him. I wanted to throw something, kick something, rip my hair out. I couldn't believe he would stoop so low. He wanted primary custody, no more 50/50. And he wanted all my visits with Meredith to be supervised. He was trying to take her away from me.

Once I was behind the wheel, all I could think of was running over Tom. I drove past him but passed just close enough for him to worry about losing his life. He jumped away and I would have smiled if I weren't so pissed off and ready to sob.

The tears came hard and fast then and I had to pull over because I was crying too hard to see. I was shaking, and I sat there for minutes sobbing until my throat and chest hurt. I told myself to knock it off. Now wasn't the time for tears. It was time for action. I picked up the phone and called my lawyer. I couldn't afford to even pay the consultation fee, I realized once I spoke to her receptionist.

What the hell am I supposed to do to see my daughter now?

I picked up the phone and called Carter.

"Can you come over?"

"I'll be right there," he said not even hesitating.

* * *

MY MIND WAS on the information in front of me as I heard Carter knock on the door ten minutes later. I'd occupied myself by looking for solutions to my issue by Googling every family lawyer I could find. I was calling offices, and most were closed.

Even though I knew what my rights were, and I knew that Tom couldn't withhold Meredith, I was still looking on every site I could find to figure out what to do next.

I was trying to figure out if I should call the cops to enforce the order when I heard a knock at my door.

I got up and went towards the door. I pulled the door open and immediately broke down again. Carter didn't say a word. He just held me as I sobbed on him.

"Whatever it is we're going to work it out."

I hoped he was right.

He ushered me back into my house and after a minute I was able to speak. Slowly, I started telling him everything. I told him about the conversation I'd had with Becca. I told him that Becca left Tom and now Tom was using Meredith to get back at me. And finally, I told him about Tom's ultimatum.

"He can't dictate who you see or what you do. As long as you're taking care of Meredith, he has no right to make demands."

"I know. I just don't know what to do."

"Do you have a lawyer? You know my stepmom would help you in a heartbeat."

"I would appreciate that. Thank you. Does she charge a lot?"

"I'm sure she'll work something out with you."

"Thanks, Carter."

"Of course. Do you want me to stay the night? So you don't have to be alone?"

I shook my head. "No. I should be fine."

As soon as he left, I passed by a mirror in my hall. I looked defeated and pitiful. I didn't want to be that person any longer. I wasn't that person any longer, so I made a game plan. I was going over to Tom's house first thing in the morning and I wasn't leaving without my daughter.

Carter called me that morning shortly after I woke up. I picked up and told him what I planned to do. He tried to convince me to call the cops, but I wanted to resolve it quickly and on my own. He tried to talk me out of it but I wasn't listening. I hung up after telling him not to come with me.

I parked my car on the street in front of Tom's house and made my way to the front door. I could see his car parked in the driveway. Good, he was home. I didn't see the maid's car and I was glad that I wouldn't have any witnesses.

I didn't hesitate. I banged on the door. Hard. Not able to control my fury.

Within seconds, he was at the door.

"Are you nuts? What are you doing here?"

"Give me back my daughter."

"Mommy?" I suddenly heard Meredith call out.

"Meredith," I called, trying to find her behind Tom.

"Go upstairs, Meredith," he ordered as he shut the door soundly behind him and stepped out to confront me.

"What the hell do you think you're doing?"

"I'm here for my daughter," I said, trying to get around him.

He grabbed my hand and slapped it off the doorknob. "Get the hell off my property or I'll call the cops."

I called his bluff. "So call them. I want you to."

I reached for the doorknob again and this time I found myself suddenly in the air and then unceremoniously dumped in the bushes next to this front porch.

Now I was furious. I struggled to get up, cursing and swearing when I tried to get my footing.

He looked at me and laughed. I finally found my footing, only to fall back down into the bushes again. Now I was even more pissed off.

I was so angry and determined to get up that I didn't even notice when Carter pulled up. I was still pulling myself up and cursing loudly when Carter strode up to the porch. He looked angrier than I was.

"Oh, here comes the cavalry," Tom said, turning towards Carter. "Get off my property, you little sh—"

He never got the other word fully out as Carter decked him once in the face. And before I knew it they were embroiled in a fight. With every punch, you could practically feel the hatred each man held for the other.

I screamed for them to stop and finally found my footing when Carter slammed Tom into his door, sending the door flying open and Tom and Carter crashing into the wall in the foyer.

They were a tangle of arms and legs. And then Carter was on top of Tom. He punched him over and over, his face showing no emotion, his punches almost robotic as they made contact with Tom's flesh.

I pulled at Carter's shirt, begging for him to stop, but it was like he didn't even hear me.

"Carter, stop, Carter!" I said, pulling at his shoulder as Tom tried to cover his face and dodge the blows that came one after another.

"Principal K," came Meredith's voice, and I instantly let go of Carter and ran to Meredith to gather her in my arms.

She buried her face in my shoulders and cried, "Please don't let him hurt Daddy."

I turned around and saw Carter climbing off Tom

and Tom angrily trying to sit up while holding his face. His nose was bleeding, saliva dribbling from his swollen lip. He was a mess.

Carter backed away looking enraged. He reached for me and I stepped away from his hand, still holding on to Meredith who looked from Carter to Tom, her eyes large and confused.

"Meredith—" Tom started to say, and Carter glared at him and he quickly shut his mouth.

"I'm taking my daughter home," I growled and walked around him.

He didn't try to stop me, and I turned around sharply when I heard footsteps behind me. It was Carter.

I didn't know I was crying then until he reached up to wipe a tear from my cheek.

"Do you want me to drive you?"

I shook my head, feeling anger, probably misplaced, towards him. I'd made a promise to Meredith to protect her and I'd been unable to do that. Her father had taken her from me. I'd failed her, and I was so angry, so disappointed in myself.

And I turned all that anger and disappointment towards Carter. "I don't want you to drive me anywhere."

He grabbed my shoulder and I shook it off.

I quickly walked with Meredith in my arms to my

car and buckled her up. Carter followed me and said, "Look, I'm sorry. I was just trying to help—"

I turned on him then. "Help? By beating her dad into a pulp in front of her?"

"I'm sorry, I didn't know she was standing there—"

"Well, she was!"

"I'm sorry. I don't know what else to say. Let me apologize to her—"

"Stay away from us," I said coldly, getting into the car. I could see Meredith crying softly in the back seat and it tore at my soul. Infuriated, I growled at Carter, "I don't care if I don't ever see you or Tom again.

He looked taken aback. "You don't mean that."

I rolled up my window and didn't bother to respond as I pulled away and drove in the direction of home.

As soon as I got home, I sent Meredith to take a bath and waited, chewing my lips for the cops to show up. I didn't know what Tom would tell them. That I attacked him? That I'd tried to force my way into his home?

But as one minute led to an hour, and an hour led to a day, I figured if he had called the cops on me, they would already have come.

I'd missed at least ten calls from Carter. But I didn't want to talk to him. My emotions were everywhere. I didn't know if I should have felt grateful to Carter for beating Tom to a pulp because I'd been a minute from trying to do the same. Or if I hated him for letting

Meredith be witness to that type of violence directed at someone she loved. I knew she loved her father even if he was deserving of every punch to the face he'd received.

She hadn't said anything about it. Nothing at all. And I hadn't put her back into school. I was too shaken. She had missed at least three days and I knew I couldn't keep her out indefinitely.

I didn't know what to do. And of course, just when I thought things couldn't get any worse. I received a letter. I was going to court. Tom had made good on his threat.

* * *

THE NEXT WEEKEND, Becca said that Tom had contacted her and asked her to take Meredith. He said it was neutral ground. I agreed, not knowing what else to do. I knew withholding Meredith would put me in contempt with the court and I didn't want Tom to have any ammo on me even though he had withheld visitation himself.

I knew I could trust Becca and so I'd let her have Meredith for the weekend. She promised that she wouldn't let her out of her sight and assured me she wouldn't let Tom go anywhere without her.

Meredith had also seemed a little frightened, but I'd assured her that Tom wouldn't dare try it again.

"Or Principal K will punch him in the face again?"

I'd looked at her in surprise and apologized for Carter.

She had shrugged. "He was just trying to protect me. And you. I love Daddy but he shouldn't have done what he did."

I'd hugged her and said, "You're right. But fighting doesn't solve anything."

She had nodded. "Yeah, he punched Daddy pretty hard. I was scared for Daddy."

"I know, hon."

"Are you still mad at Principal K?"

"Mad? No. I just... I don't know."

"He really likes you, Mom. He just made a mistake."

And that was the conversation she left me with.

I didn't go home. I didn't want to be alone. I sat in my car sniffling, and then called Piper. "Can I come over?"

She didn't even hesitate.

"Of course."

About fifteen minutes later, I was knocking at her door.

"It's open," she called. "Magic man never locked it."

"The magician was here?" I asked, curious.

"Yeah."

"This early in the morning?"

"He spent the night."

My eyes widened. "Seriously?"

She sat down across from me and said, "He's great but I don't see things working out between us. His career is just so demanding."

I looked at her and my expression must have been dubious.

"Well, it is! He's always doing birthday parties or traveling to one party or another. I rarely get to see him."

"Wow, I didn't think a magician's world was so intense."

She sighed sadly. "You have no idea. It's like he's a military officer instead of just some dude who pulls rabbits out of his hat."

"I'm sorry," I said, trying to sound sincere, but I thought she could do better than a magician.

"It's okay. Onto the next one," she said with forced cheer and then her eyes grew serious, "But we're not here to talk about me. Tell me what's going on."

I filled her in, leaving out nothing. She was quiet the whole time and then said, "I think you and Carter need to talk."

I nodded.

"He's always hated Tom, rightfully so. Tom was always a controlling bastard. He used to hold my Barbies hostage. But he was mom's favorite so he never got in trouble for anything. He made my life a living hell."

"Ditto," I said.

"But holding Barbie hostage is one thing, holding a kid from her mom is some prime A bullshit."

I nodded and said, "And now he's taking me to court."

She reached across the table and took my hand and squeezed it. "If you need anything, you tell me, okay?"

I laughed. "You know a good lawyer?"

"I don't, but Carter does… speaking of which, he should be here any minute now."

"What?" I said. "You told Carter I was here?"

"I did. I hate that my two best friends aren't speaking to each other."

I shook my head. "Piper, I don't know. I'm just so emotional now, I'm just not ready to talk to him."

"Too late," she said, looking over my shoulder and through her front window. "He's here. I'll give you two some privacy."

She stood up, grabbed her purse, put on some sunglasses and disappeared through her door.

"See you guys," she said happily as she bounced past a startled Carter.

We both watched as she climbed into her car and drove off.

"Why haven't you returned any of my calls?" he asked immediately.

"I've had a lot on my mind and didn't know what to say."

"Listen, I'm sorry for what happened. I'm not sorry for punching Tom, but I am sorry that I did it in front of Meredith."

"Okay."

"Okay is all you have to say?"

"What do you want me to say?"

"I don't know. You could say that you forgive me."

I shook my head. "I don't know how I feel. I really don't. I just think right now our emotions are raw and I don't want to say anything that I'll regret, but I think we should take a break."

He looked like I'd hit him. The shock that registered on his face…

"A break? We just started seeing each other."

"I know," I said, looking down unable to face him. "I just feel like maybe me and you, like maybe this was a mistake… things just went so fast and got complicated so soon."

"So you regret what happened with us?"

"No. Yes. I don't know. I just can't handle this—us— right now. I just can't. Tom's taking me to court and I just don't want to complicate things right now."

"So that's it then?"

His voice was quiet, and I forced myself to look at him. He was trying to hide it but I could tell my words hurt him. I swallowed hard, trying to hold back tears, but hoping that I was doing the right thing. I desperately hoped I knew what I was doing. Wasn't this best for everybody? For Meredith? For me?

"I just know how bitter and mean Tom can be. I don't want him to destroy your career and I think I'm confusing Meredith."

"You can stop with the excuses. I get it." He stood up.

"I'm just looking out for you and Meredith."

"You don't have to explain... I get it." His tone was bitter, and I found myself getting upset. I was feeling judged and so I lashed out.

"Why are you angry with me? I'm just doing what I think is best."

"I'm tired of hearing the same excuse. I heard it eight years ago and you're using the same excuse now. I'm not sure why I convinced myself that this time would be different. I'm not sure why I even tried."

"You're one to talk. You haven't even been around for almost a decade. You were supposed to be my best friend but you left. I needed you and you left." My voice cracked. And now we were getting to the truth of the matter.

"I left because I couldn't stand seeing you married to him. It was hard enough to know you went back to him after being in my arms and you expected me to just accept it."

"We were friends, Carter. I didn't want to mess up what we had by letting our mess up, well, mess things up," I said, sounding desperate. My voice was already feeling raw.

"Mess things up? Do you know how I felt after you literally went from my bed to seeking him out?"

I gulped. "He was my boyfriend. What did you expect me to do? I woke up that morning and realized that I'd a made a mistake."

He shook his head. "You considered us a mistake?"

"Yes!" I said too strongly, but my nerves were raw and my emotions were everywhere. I didn't know. "I was embarrassed and ashamed about what we'd done."

He stared at me in silence, and the judgment I felt made me tear up.

"You felt ashamed? Sorry that being with me made you feel ashamed. I didn't know you'd felt that way."

He stood up and turned and walked towards the door.

"Where are you going?"

"I'm leaving. I don't want to give you a reason to feel ashamed again."

"Carter—"

"You've said enough, Dana. More than enough."

"Don't leave."

But he was already gone.

I put my face in my hands and tried to just breathe. But I couldn't think of anything but that night I'd slept with Carter and then left.

It had been cowardly of me. I hadn't even left him a note. I'd just snuck out of his bed that morning while he was in the shower and made my way back to my dorm where I'd found Tom sitting there.

He'd confessed that he'd cheated. He told me that he hadn't gone all the way with her. And of course, I hadn't believed him, but I didn't have a backbone. I'd felt guilty for what I'd done with Carter, but more than that I'd felt guilty that all the time I'd been with Tom, I'd always been in love with Carter.

And then to my surprise, Tom had asked me to marry him right then and there. He got down on one knee and proposed. And the ring had been a family heirloom. His proposal represented everything I thought I wanted in life.

And I'd found myself saying yes. As he'd hugged me, I'd wondered if he could smell the scent of Carter on my flesh. If I closed my eyes long enough, I could still feel the way he touched me and caressed me.

A few hours later, Carter had stopped by my dorm and he'd found Tom there. And I'll never forget the look on Carter's face as Tom referred to me as the future Mrs. Duran and told me to show Carter the ring.

Carter's face had registered shock and the hurt I saw in his eyes when he looked up at me made me so sick, I felt my stomach clench.

"Congratulations," he'd said softly and then he'd walked away. I'd never forgot the look on Tom's face either. He had looked… victorious.

Part of me died that day. I'd been ashamed of what I'd done with Carter but I hadn't regretted it.

I looked for him and found him in the library. I'd tried to apologize to him, but he hadn't wanted to hear an apology and he'd quickly changed the subject. He was still friendly, but I knew that our act and my accepting of Tom's proposal had changed things between us. There was no going back.

The last time I'd seen him before he'd left the country, had been at my wedding. He'd danced with me. And I remember thinking how I'd wished it had been Carter as my groom even then. But I'd buried that memory because it had made me feel guilty… guilty that even at my own wedding, I'd been thinking of what it would be like to be married to Carter.

And now I would never know.

I stood up and walked to Piper's couch. I tossed my feet up, buried my head under a throw pillow and sobbed.

My life was a mess. And I had no one to blame but myself.

11

"Mom, check this out. I can do a cartwheel," Meredith said as she quickly executed the perfect cartwheel.

"Good job," I said, reaching out to high-five her. "You're so awesome."

"So are you," she said as she started doing cartwheels across the yard. I sat there and watched her and just felt insanely grateful about how things had turned out.

I retained primary custody of Meredith. Tom hadn't gotten what he wanted. We were still on an every other weekend and one day a week schedule. The judge had also made us attend a mediation class which had made Tom angry, but ultimately had been good for the both of us. We'd pretty much come to an agreement to mind our own business. I wouldn't interfere in his life and he wouldn't interfere in mine.

My lawyer had been awesome, the perfect advocate. If it wasn't for her, I'm sure Tom's fancy lawyer would have torn me to pieces.

I had Carter to thank but he still wasn't speaking to me. It had been three months since he'd come by Piper's house to see me.

If it hadn't been for his stepmom acting as my attorney pro-bono, I don't know what I would have done. She had called me that same day when Carter walked out of my life and even though I'd been a mess emotionally, I'd managed to keep it together long enough to tell her the situation. She had readily agreed to help. It had been like a weight being lifted off my shoulder.

But I didn't feel so light now. I felt lonely and sad. I missed Carter so much. I thought about him literally every night. I found myself daydreaming at my job, wondering what he was doing and if he missed me too.

I didn't see him anymore when I dropped Meredith off at school and Meredith had sadly informed me that he had resigned. Piper told me that he was looking for a position elsewhere. I knew I was partially responsible for that. Maybe fully responsible.

He didn't want anything to do with me, so he was going out of his way to make sure he didn't have to see me, even if that meant letting go of a job he loved.

When I'd heard, I'd felt so guilty. I'd summoned the

courage to call him to tell him how sorry I was, but he never answered. All my calls went straight to voicemail.

So, I just went through the motions, glad that he had cared enough about me, even after I'd rejected him, to get me a lawyer, but at the same time so upset that he wasn't talking to me and it seemed he never planned to again.

I felt like I was missing a part of myself. I didn't know what to do. I'd shed quite a few tears and I missed him with my whole heart. I sent emails, made phone calls, left messages with Piper to deliver to him, but there was nothing but silence.

But what had I expected? He'd loved me and had been loyal to me since we first met, but how had I treated that love? And how many times had I pushed him away? I was good at hurting him and I didn't blame him for not wanting to be around me anymore. I was toxic.

He'd only ever shown me love and friendship and what had I offered to him in return? Drama. Shame. More drama.

I guess I spent a bit too much time feeling sorry for myself because suddenly Meredith was sitting next to me looking at me inquiringly.

"You miss him, don't you?" she said softly.

I knew it would be useless to be coy. There was no fooling Meredith and it was about time that I was honest with how I was feeling instead of pretending everything was fine.

"I miss him a lot," I said simply.

"Why don't you call him?"

"He doesn't want to speak to me. I tried calling him."

She frowned. "What did you do? Why is he angry with you? Did you yell at him for beating up Daddy?"

I nodded. "Kind of. And I told him that I didn't want him around."

She gasped. "Why'd you do that?"

I shrugged and then sighed deeply. "I don't know. I was upset and emotional. And he had beat up your father—"

"Well, Dad did dump you in the bushes, so he did deserve to get punched in the face."

I didn't know what to say, so I said nothing.

"Principal K, I mean Carter, would never dump you in the bushes, he loves you too much."

"Loved. I'm sure he doesn't love me anymore."

She laughed and that made me look at her in surprise. "If someone really loves you, they can't just stop loving you, Mom. That's not how love works. Auntie Piper said that Carter has loved you since college. He's not going to just stop loving you now because you guys had a little fight."

"Well, it wasn't exactly a little fight."

"Stop making excuses, Mom. If you love Carter, just

go over to his house to tell him. You went to Daddy's house to get me back. You were really brave. You can do it again. Just go to Carter's house and say, 'I'm sorry I dumped you. I love you. I want you back.'"

"What if he doesn't want to be with me anymore?"

She looked at me as if I were stupid. "Then I guess you'll just have to hang out in bars with Becca. She told me she hates the bar scene but she doesn't know where else to find guys."

"Becca said that?"

She nodded. I made a mental note to tell Becca to stop talking about bars with Meredith.

"Well, Becca has a point. How about I call her and have her watch you for an hour while I run over to Carter's place?"

She nodded happily. "Sounds like a plan."

Before I could lose my nerve, I picked up the phone and called Becca. She promptly arrived ten minutes later.

"Go get 'em, tiger," she said to me as I grabbed my purse and looked in the mirror one last time before heading out the door.

I smiled and hoped I appeared confident, but I wasn't. I was scared he wouldn't open the door to speak with me. I was afraid he'd just ignore me. Or worse, I was afraid he'd tell me he didn't love me anymore.

So, as I drove up and parked in front of his car, I was a big ball of fear.

And of course, I found him shirtless, working in his garden. He had on a baseball cap and low riding shorts.

I couldn't help but stare at his chest. He was still beautiful. Apparently, he hadn't fallen into a bucket of ice cream after I dumped him. I couldn't say the same about myself, I thought as I sucked in my tummy and straightened my shoulders.

"Come on, Dana. You can do this." I gave myself a little pep talk before I opened the door and stepped out.

He looked up at my car but didn't acknowledge me. He just kept working in his garden. I stood at the gate that led to his walkway and waited for him to say something, anything to me.

"I see you're busy," I said with a shaky voice. "Want to take a break for a moment to talk?"

"No," he said, not even turning around to face me.

I instantly wanted to run back to the car and hide, but I was done running from Carter. I was a grown woman and it was time that I started acting like one.

I opened the gate and walked up the walkway and stood next to him. "Look, can you at least hear me out?"

"I'd rather not," he said as he continued working. I watched how quickly his hands moved over the area in front of him, pulling weeds quickly and efficiently. While I thought of what to say my eyes wandered over the entire garden. Everything was in bloom. I could smell the jasmines again and he'd installed little lights around the perimeter in various sites. The sun was going down and the lights were starting to turn on. I guessed that they were solar powered.

I turned my eyes back on him and thought about all the time he must have dedicated to his garden. He was patient. Good at nurturing things. He was a natural caretaker. Persistent, gentle, forgiving. Everything I wasn't, but everything that his love had taught me to be.

I squatted down next to him, in my little sundress and heels. "Can I help?"

He still didn't look at me, he just stood up abruptly and walked to his garage. I stood there awkwardly, wondering if that was my sign to leave.

I was turning away when he reappeared suddenly with an extra pair of gloves. "Here," he said, still avoiding eye contact as he handed them to me.

He didn't say another word. He just silently worked in his garden. I watched him for a second then got on my knees in the dirt and started weeding his flower bed.

We worked in silence until finally, it was driving me crazy. "I wanted to thank you for having your stepmom represent me in court. She was amazing. She pretty much crushed Tom's lawyer."

He grunted and busily spread some mulch. "She's a force to be reckoned with."

"Yeah," I said, not knowing what else to say. "Well, we won in court. I still have primary custody."

"That's great."

I stared at him waiting for him to say something else, but nothing came. I took a deep breath and decided to just tell him what was in my heart.

"Listen, I know that I said many things that hurt you and I'm really sorry. I'm a coward, Carter. I was scared of just being happy. You know what my mom said to me once?" When he didn't say anything I continued, "She said that no one is actually happy. She said we're all discontent in life, that discontentment is just the human condition. She said that certain things could make us temporarily content, but otherwise there was no such thing as happiness."

He still continued to work, not saying anything, so I pressed on.

"I think I really believed that. I really believed that happiness wasn't in the cards for me, so every time I had the opportunity to be truly happy I freaked out because I was so scared that it wouldn't last." I touched his shoulder and said, "Look at me."

Finally, he did. His eyes were emotionless and guarded. His mouth was drawn into a tight line. Clearly, I wasn't getting anywhere. He was still shutting me out.

"I'm not scared anymore. I mean I was before." I shook my head and then raised my eyes to his. "But I knew all those years ago that being around you, just being with you made me happy. And I know that I want to spend the rest of my life with you, happy and secure in the fact that you love me. I want that chance, Carter. I know I probably don't deserve it, but I desperately want that chance to be happy with you again. I love you so much—" My voice cracked but I pressed on even though he continued to look at me coldly, unmoved by my words.

I tried again. "I love you so much. You mean so much to me and I just want to tell you that I'm sorry for what happened three months ago. The things I said. And I'm sorry for what happened eight years ago. I mean, I'm not apologizing for what we did. I'm just apologizing for how I left things… for how I hurt you."

I reached for his hand and squeezed it. "I'm asking for your forgiveness. And for a second, or I guess now it's a third chance." I gave a nervous laugh and he finally broke eye contact and turned away from me and started again to work.

"I have to finish this. Thanks for stopping by, Dana," was all he said.

I couldn't even speak. He was rejecting me. It was over. History was repeating itself. I was going to lose Carter yet again.

Feeling numb, I got into my car and drove home. I pulled up in front of my house and just sat there in shock. Then the tears came. I leaned my head on the wheel and just cried until no more tears were left. I'd gambled and lost. He didn't want my love. I'd hurt him too much.

With shaky legs, I climbed out of the car, opened my front door and walked into my house. I saw Becca and Meredith sitting there watching some TV show about wedding dresses.

"You're thinking of getting married again?" I said incredulously.

Becca shrugged. "You know what they say. Once you fall off a horse, you just climb back on."

"Marriage isn't a horse."

"Well… yeah… So how did things go between you and—" She abruptly stopped. "Never mind. The look on your face tells all. I'm sorry."

I tried to smile bravely but I failed. Instead I mumbled, "I'll be in my room if you need me."

Meredith was sleeping or she would have been full of questions too. I made my way to my room and fell into a deep sleep. I'd finally found out what it felt like to be loved and cherished. I'd been a happy woman and I'd thrown it all away.

IT WAS dark when I woke up and I could hear the TV on in the background. I pulled myself out of my slumber and almost screamed when I caught a glimpse of myself in the mirror. I looked crazy. Maybe I'd fought myself in my sleep, I thought, running a hand through my hair.

I checked on Meredith and realized that Becca had put her to bed. Becca left me a note saying that she hoped I felt better. She was truly a sweet person.

I then practically jumped out of my skin when I heard the doorbell ring. I picked up an umbrella ready to clobber the person on the other side of the door when I realized it was Carter.

I opened it, confused.

He looked at me and then the umbrella and said, "I guess you weren't expecting me?"

I was confused and surprised. "Should I be?"

"You texted me."

"No, I didn't."

He pulled his phone out of his pocket and read it out loud to me. "I have an emergency. Please stop by."

I shook my head. "I didn't text you. I couldn't have. I just woke up."

And then I sighed. "I'm going to guess that text came from Meredith."

He chuckled. "I should have guessed that. Please was misspelled. I just thought you were too busy handling an emergency to notice."

We awkwardly stood there staring at each other when finally, I said, "Well, thanks for coming over. You're always running to my rescue…" I let my voice trail off and whispered, "Even when you hate me…"

"I don't hate you," he said, and I gave him a dubious look.

"You could barely look at me a few hours ago."

"You surprised me. That's all. I didn't really know how to feel. But I don't hate you. I could never hate you."

He reached for me then and pulled me towards him.

I let him pull me into his arms and I lay my head against his chest. Everything about being held by Carter just felt right.

"I love you too much to hate you," he whispered against my hair.

I tightened my arms around him and tilted my face up to look into his eyes. "I'm so sorry for everything. I'm especially sorry that you felt it was necessary to leave your job."

"It would have been hell seeing you every day knowing that you didn't feel for me like I felt for you. Last time that happened I left the country and didn't come back. This time I figured I would stay in the country and just find another job."

"I'm glad then that you only quit your job and didn't leave America just because I'm the world's biggest idiot."

"I don't know. I would argue that you don't have that

title… yet," he said, placing his hands on either side of my face. "But there's a title I would like you to hold… how does Mrs. Knight sound to you?"

I blinked and realized I had tears in my eyes. Tears of joy. "I think that's a title I would like to have."

"Finally!" someone said behind us, and I turned around to see Meredith smiling.

"I know you sent that text, missy," I said, giving her a stern look, but unable to hold back a smile.

"Someone had to help you two out. You guys are terrible communicators."

I looked at Carter, Carter looked at me, and we both laughed. Meredith skipped over to join us and wrapped her arms around our waists as best as she could.

"Are you guys going to get married?" she asked hopefully.

We nodded at the same time. Meredith looked relieved. "Great. I really want a little brother. And maybe a little sister. Maybe even twins."

I looked at Carter and he looked at me. The shock was apparent on both of our faces. "How about we start with planning the wedding first?"

Meredith shrugged. "I guess… but you don't need a wedding to have a baby." She gave us a serious look and said, "You guys do know how babies are made, right?"

Carter and I instantly let go of each other and I knew I was turning as red as he was.

"How about you just go back to bed?"

She shrugged happily. "I'm just glad I'm going to get a little brother or sister or both before Danny Schultz. His mom won't even go out on a date. Danny said his mom is afraid of her own shadow."

I stifled a giggle. "Goodnight, Meredith."

"Goodnight mom, Goodnight ex-Principal K."

"Night, Meredith."

When she closed the door behind her, Carter again brought me into his arms. "You sure you want to be a part of all this?"

He smiled and kissed me hard on my lips. He pulled back and said, "I wouldn't have it any other way."

And as we stood on my porch, holding each other, I knew then what true happiness meant. My mom had been wrong. Love and happiness went hand in hand. I was unconditionally and whole-heartedly loved by this man and I knew that because of his love, every day of my life would be full of happiness.

"I love you, Carter," I whispered against his ear, "But I really hope we don't have twins."

He threw his head back and laughed. "Even if we do I can't imagine a more amazing person to have children with. I love you too."

We stood there in each other's arms. And I knew that both of us were envisioning a future together. A future full of laughter, happiness, and plenty of love.

"Mom, take a picture of me. Come on, Mom," Meredith said pulling at my shoulder.

"Give me one sec. I just need to get this diaper—" I didn't get another word out as the diaper came flying up and hit me squarely in the face.

Meredith immediately burst into laughter, holding on to her side. "Oh my God, you should have seen your face. Hilarious."

Meredith sighed. "Next time duck, Mom. Move on over, let me help. You go sit down. You need a break. And I'm an expert. I can change a diaper in thirty seconds flat."

She did exactly that. I barely had time to collapse on the bed before she was done.

"Oh, my amazing girl, what did I ever do right in life

to deserve you?" I said, closing my eyes as I sank down into the pillows. I just needed a nap. Just one minute, that was all I needed.

"Umph" I groaned as something that felt like a sack of potatoes landed on my back and knocked the wind out of me.

Meredith laughed. "Gabby, you're too funny."

"All my children are trying to kill me," I said with my eyes still closed, determined to get just a few seconds of a nap.

"Just Gabby. CJ just wanted you to change his diaper faster."

I opened my eyes and the three of them stood there looking at me with goofy faces. My twins had just turned a year old. I had a girl, Gabrielle, and a son, Carter Jr. We called him CJ for short. CJ was pretty tame and pretty much slept and played quietly by himself. Gabrielle, or better known as Gabby, was bold, adventurous and always getting into trouble.

They all looked at me with goofy looks on their faces and I couldn't help but smile back. "Come here, you guys,"

I held my arms out and they jumped into them. And that's how Carter found me when he walked into our room.

"Another group hug without me?" he asked.

He didn't need to say another word as they switched

gears and piled on him instead, almost knocking him on his butt.

"Woah, woah, woah," Carter said, falling over as he tried to steady himself. "I guess you guys missed me?"

They all nodded in unison and held him tighter. I pulled myself up on my elbows and looked at them. Who would have thought that three years ago, my life would end up here?

Carter and I had married less than a week after he'd proposed. It had just felt right. We figured, why wait? We'd already loved each other for what felt like a lifetime.

He'd reapplied for his old job and was reinstated as principal at the International School. Meredith loved having two dads. And for the sake of Meredith, Tom was always on his best behavior. Mostly, he was afraid of Carter's stepmom taking him to court.

Tom was also on his third divorce, but already had a new girlfriend. Even Meredith was starting to mix their names up. Becca was still a constant figure in our lives. In fact, we were on our way to her college graduation.

She had earned her bachelor's degree in record time and was thinking of continuing on to law school to study family law. Becca spent the weekends with us sometimes and she was more like the little sister I'd never had. We'd become such good friends and it was hard to think that I could have ever thought to dislike her. She was funny, caring, a little ditzy, but a great person. She had even become a doula so that she could help me when I went into labor with the twins. I thought she would pass out at the first sign of labor, but she had held up even better than Carter. In fact, she'd had to give Carter a pep talk.

And she'd taken care of Meredith during the time when I was in the hospital after having the twins.

I had to give a lot of credit to Meredith. She was a champ and it seemed the bigger our family got, the happier she was.

She immediately accepted Carter and was terribly excited about the twins. She wasn't excited about the additional chores, but she was a champion diaper changer and she frequently got up before I did to get the babies a bottle in the middle of the night. She was the best big sister, but I knew she would be.

Carter pulled the twins off him, gave them a kiss on the forehead and then turned to Meredith and said, "Why don't you go ahead and get ready? I'll take care of these two troublemakers."

"Thanks, Carter," she said, before skipping away.

At first, she had tried to call Carter "Dad" but it had gotten awkward, so they had both agreed that Carter was just fine. He respected the fact that Tom was her father and he didn't try to interfere with their rela-tionship.

I moved to get up but Carter stopped me. "Take a nap. You look tired. I'll get the kids ready and then wake you up."

He kissed me softly on the lips and my eyes closed and I fell asleep. I don't know how long I was out, but I felt him shaking my shoulder gently.

"Hey sleepyhead," he said once my eyes were open. "Put these on and meet us downstairs. We'll wait for you in the car."

I looked around and not only were all the kids dressed, but the nursery was organized, and Carter had picked out something for me to wear so that I wouldn't even need to think about it.

That was life with Carter. He made everything so much easier. He anticipated my needs before I did, and I was so grateful to have such a loving partner in life.

For what felt like the millionth time, I thanked Tom in my head for divorcing me. He had done me a huge favor. If he hadn't divorced me, I wouldn't be surrounded now by so much love.

I took a quick shower to wake up, brushed my teeth, and then slipped into my clothes. I grabbed an apple on the way out and locked the door behind me. We were all living in Carter's craftsman style home and we'd made an addition to it to make room for the twins.

I walked past the garden that Meredith now helped

Carter with every Saturday and saw that the plants they'd planted were already sprouting.

I jumped in the car and Carter gave a low whistle. "You look amazing."

"I feel like I was hit by a pile of bricks."

"Sexy bricks," Carter reassured me as he backed out.

Meredith laughed.

The twins were busy playing with some sort of toy Carter gave them to distract themselves and we arrived at the college where graduation was being held in no time.

We found our seats. Piper and her latest boyfriend joined us. I think he was an acrobat or some guy she'd met while taking Meredith to see the circus. I also got a chance to meet Becca's dad. He was a nice guy, shy and a little anxious.

We all sat next to each other and clapped enthusiastically when Becca's name was announced. After the ceremony, we eagerly anticipated her arrival and waited in the hall for her to appear.

She came towards us a few minutes later, laughing and hugging friends. I don't think I saw her any happier.

When she saw us she squeaked, waved and flew towards us. Her dad caught her in a big hug and then Meredith hugged her as well. The twins followed suit because of course, they wanted to do whatever their big sister did.

"Congratulations," I said as I finally got a chance to embrace her.

"Thanks for being here," she said. "It means a lot."

"I'm starving," said Meredith suddenly, "Let's take this party elsewhere."

"Sounds like a plan to me," I said.

We wrangled the twins and put them back in the stroller. Meredith happily pushed them along while she walked between Becca and her father, chatting. She was such a social butterfly. She loved new people.

Carter slid his hand into mine and we walked hand in hand behind our blended family.

"Thank you," he said suddenly, stopping me while the others walked on.

"For what?" I asked turning to look at him.

"For giving me such a beautiful family. None of this was possible without you." His eyes locked with mine and I couldn't help but smile. I was so lucky that Carter had decided to love me.

"Maybe I should be thanking you…"

"You gave birth to twins—"

"You're right. I deserve ALL the thanks."

He laughed and then pulled me close. "I love you, Dana."

"The feeling's mutual," I joked, and as he laughed, I kissed him, knowing that our lives together would be like this moment every day: Full of love and laughter.

BONUS SEX SCENE: DORM ROOM

As he undressed me, I couldn't even think. All I could hear were the sounds of someone in a neighboring room blasting hip-hop with so much bass it made the walls shake.

I figured that was a good thing because if his kiss was any indication, his touch was going to set me on fire too and I would be moaning and screaming his name in record time.

His mouth was back on mine as he finally undressed me and led me to his bed. He stepped out of his pants and lay me down.

I reached for him, but he pushed my hand away and instead, lay down next to me. In the narrow bed, he was pressed against the wall and he leaned over and started placing kisses down my belly. He kissed my belly button and I let out a nervous giggle.

But my giggles ceased as he trailed kisses further and further south until he was kissing my sex. I sucked in a breath. He gently parted my legs, pushing my thighs apart to gain further access. I was shy, but I let him, gasping as his tongue licked my folds.

I'd never had a man do that to me before and I didn't know how I felt about it. As his tongue brushed against my clit, I quickly changed my mind. I knew exactly how I felt about it. I liked it. And I wanted him to never stop.

"Don't stop," I said growing bolder and spreading my legs wider on the narrow twin bed to give him better access.

He moved then and kneeled between my legs to bring himself closer. I wantonly gripped his head and rode his mouth, rotating my hips against his lips as he sucked and licked my clit, my folds, and then penetrated me with his tongue, teasing my entryway until I was wet and dripping.

He reached past me and opened a drawer. I realized he was putting on a condom. He quickly sheathed himself and then wrapped my legs around his hips.

His body was against mine and I could feel his sex nudging at my folds. I greedily tried to rub against him, trying to tip my hips up so that he was inside of me.

But he was determined to take his time.

"Open your eyes," he said, and not until that moment did I realize they were closed.

Slowly, I opened them, and he took that moment to stroke the side of my face. And then with his eyes holding mine, he moved his hips and slid slowly into me.

My breath caught, and I tossed my head back as he filled me and stretched me. My wetness tugged at him and he groaned and began to kiss my neck as he moved inside of me.

It had only been a moment, but I was so turned on that I instantly began to come.

"Already?" I heard him joke as my body began to shudder, and a scream tore from my mouth. He tried to smother it by kissing me, but it was too late.

Someone pounded on the wall next to us, but I was beyond caring. I didn't care if the whole campus heard us.

Tom had never made me feel as good as Carter did. Sex with Tom had always been passionless and robotic. And now I knew that was probably because he was getting it from someone else, someone probably more experienced and sexier than me.

But Carter made me feel sexy and desirable. As he continued to move inside me, I could feel my inner muscles clenching around him, holding him and squeezing him with every thrust.

He seemed to like it, I noticed. And I laughed, feeling

powerful and wanton. Two emotions I wasn't used to feeling while making love.

And I wondered if this was what it was for Carter. Instead of just sex. After all, when he said he loved me I believed him, because whether I admitted it out loud or not, I deeply loved him too.

With that thought in mind, I focused on letting my body say the words I couldn't speak. I let my hands wander across his shoulders, memorizing the feel of his warm skin against my palms. I dug my heels into this backside, wanting to feel him deeper inside me.

And then I motioned for him to lean forward so that I could kiss him as he pumped into me, taking his time, as if he could do this forever.

He pulled away just far enough to fondle my breasts and then he pulled one of my nipples into his mouth.

"Carter," I gasped, and he continued sucking on it until it was hard and straining towards him.

With every tug of his mouth on my nipple, my sex clenched around him and before long, I was close to coming again. And I knew he was close too as his pace quickened and his thrusts deepened.

"God, you feel so good," he moaned. And then we came together, me shaking and moaning. And Carter burying himself into me one last time before grunting and collapsing against me. He wrapped his arms around me and rolled a little to his side so that his weight wouldn't be too much for me. And we lay like that connected, just breathing. My head was pressed against his chest and I brought my hand up and just traced it across his shoulder.

"Did you mean what you said?"

"When I said that I loved you?"

I nodded, suddenly too filled with emotion to speak.

He stroked a hand over my cheek and then lowered his head to briefly kiss me on my lips.

"I love you now, Dana. And I'll love you forever."

I didn't know what to say, so I buried my head against his chest and let him just hold me. I knew in the light of day I would have to handle what I'd just done, but that evening I pushed all thoughts of Tom, infidelity —mine and his—away. Tonight, I just wanted to know what it felt like to be loved and desired.

I said in a whisper against his chest with a boldness I wasn't used to feeling, "Do you want to do it again?"

His eyes shot open in surprise and I could feel him hardening inside of me again. I guess that was my answer.

He reached for another condom and pulled out of me, quickly got rid of the old one and sheathed himself with the new one. I parted my legs and embraced him, groaning as he pushed inside of me, filling me with his heat, and his love.

DARK DESIRES

~ A billionaire dark romance series ~

Dark Desire

Dark Rules

Dark Secret

Dark Time

Dark Truth

BARRE TO BAR

~ A billionaire second chance series ~

Dancing With Lies

Dancing With Temptation

Dancing With Doubt

Dancing With Guilt

Dancing With Redemption

TWISTED INTENTION
~ A billionaire revenge romance series ~
Twisted Beauty
Twisted Love
Twisted Fate

Mafia's Obsession
~ A hot mafia romance series ~
Mafia's Dirty Secret
Mafia's Fake Bride
Mafia's Final Play

Screaming Demons
~ An MC romance series full of suspense ~
Rough Start
Rough Ride
Rough Choice
Rough Patch
Rough Return
Rough Road
Rough Trip
Rough Night
Rough Love

Standalone Contemporary Romance
Billionaire in Vegas
Billionaire Hunt

Billionaire's Game
Billionaire Retreat
Billionaire On Air
A Chance To Love
Somebody To Love
Not Mine To Love

Check out Summer's entire collection at
www.summercooper.com/books

ABOUT SUMMER COOPER

Thank you so much for reading. Without you, it wouldn't be possible for me to be a full-time author. I hope you enjoy reading my books as much as I do writing them.

Besides (obviously!) reading and writing, I also love cuddling my dogs, shouting at Alexa, being upside down (aka Yoga) and driving my family cray-cray!

Get in touch at
hello@summercooper.com
www.summercooper.com

facebook.com/summercooperauthor
instagram.com/summercooperauthor
goodreads.com/summercooper
bookbub.com/profile/summer-cooper